THE TIME BANDIT

Barry Cole

http://www.elbapublishing.co.uk

Dedication

To Dylan

Acknowledgements

MY THANKS GO to Daniella Foltz of Morphy Auctions for giving her permission for a photograph from their auction catalogue to be featured on the front cover of the book and to Claire Manion and her son Dylan for proofing the original manuscript and for their constructive suggestions and editing skills, for which I am truly grateful.

Contents

Chapter One

Followed

SAM AND LIZZIE knew someone was following them. They had first caught sight of him as they came out from the spinney behind the Abbott's farmhouse and again as they cut across the meadow where Mr Abbott grazed his two horses. Most worrying of all was the fact that he seemed quite unconcerned that they were aware of his presence. Lengthening their stride and keeping to the rutted track, which ran alongside a tall hedgerow, the two youngsters made a beeline for the cluster of houses in the distance. With arms and legs flying they raced down a steep hillside known locally as "The Slope" on account of it being used as a toboggan run on the rare occasions when there was a sufficient fall of snow. At the foot of the hill lay their final obstacle, the rusting remains of tall wrought iron railings, which ran alongside a disused railway line. Quick as a flash, Lizzie hitched up her dress and tucking it into her knickers, she scaled the railings with ease and dropped down safely on the other side. Agile as a monkey Sam followed after her and reaching the top, he paused for a moment to cast an anxious look behind him.

'He's still following us,' said Sam, jumping down from the fence, 'what do we do now?'

Lizzie stared thoughtfully for a minute and then her freckled face lit up with a smile.

'Follow me,' she said excitedly 'I know just the place to hide.' And with that she raced away with Sam hot on her heels.

Trudging along the narrow track PC Goodrich began to regret answering the telephone, ruefully aware that if he hadn't picked up the receiver, he would still be back in his snug little office at the local police station enjoying a nice cup of tea, instead of gallivanting around the countryside on some wild goose chase. Reaching the end of the track and seeing his quarry disappear below the crest of the hill, PC Goodrich quickly pushed such thoughts aside and reminded himself that a crime had been committed and although it only involved the theft of a few apples, as the local constable it was his duty to investigate the matter and apprehend those responsible.

He was also very aware that the person who had made the phone call was none other than Miss Litchetwood, chairperson of the Parish Council and a lady who you definitely didn't want to get on the wrong side of. His predecessor had made that mistake and as a result he was now back pounding the beat in Fordingham. No, the position of Tingwick village constable suited PC Goodrich very well and the last thing he wanted was to put it in jeopardy. So on reflection, answering the telephone had been a wise decision after all as apprehending the perpetrators of the crime would put him in Miss Litchetwood's good books and that was not a bad thing at all.

Pushing his bicycle and quite out of breath he reached the top of "The Slope" just in time to see the two youngsters climb the railings and race away. He considered free-wheeling down the steep hill in pursuit but after viewing the phalanx of rusting railings and imagining for one horrible moment being impaled on their spear-like spikes he decided against it. Besides he reminded himself, there was really no need for him to hurry, after all he had a pretty good idea where his two suspects were heading for. In fact he would bet a week's wages on it.

Chapter Two

The Scrap Yard

VASS'S SCRAP YARD lay on the far side of the village behind what remained of the old railway sidings, its piles of rusting metal and abandoned cars concealed behind a high corrugated iron fence, its panels coated in a thick layer of black paint. Once a thriving concern, with the closure of the main railway line the supply of scrap metal had dried up and the business quickly went into decline with the result that today there was barely enough work to keep old Mr Vass and his one employee occupied.

Some years earlier when the station buildings which had conveniently screened the scrap yard from the village were demolished, a petition had been organised by a group of newcomers to the village to have the yard closed down on environmental grounds – the real reason being that they thought that such an eye sore would put off potential buyers when they came to sell their properties. Thankfully for Mr Vass, the older residents, with memories of when the scrap yard had provided much needed employment for husbands and sons returning from the war, expressed their gratitude by successfully opposing the closure. As a compromise the Parish Council approved the payment from parish funds for the planting of a row of conifers to screen the yard from view but sadly due to the soil having been contaminated over the years by pollutants seeping into the ground from the yard, the conifers quickly withered and died. As it was deemed impractical to replace them with new trees, it was suggested to Mr Vass that to improve the appearance of the scrap yard, he might consider applying a coat of paint – several if necessary – to the corrugated iron fence which enclosed the yard. Thankfully and much to the relief of all concerned, Mr Vass complied with the request and so brought the matter to a close.

Lizzie and Sam crossed the tracks of the old spur line which had once allowed flat-bed trucks to be shunted into the scrap yard from the main line and made their way alongside the high corrugated iron fence, with Lizzie counting each panel as they went.

'Where are we going?' Sam enquired, 'and why are you....', 'shush,' snapped Lizzie, 'can't you see I'm counting?'

Sam shrugged his shoulders and gave a small smile. He and Lizzie had been friends ever since his family moved into the house next door to hers two years ago so he knew from experience that eventually she would reveal why they were wandering around the outside of the scrap yard instead of just sneaking in through the front gates, which he had noticed were wide open and unattended. He didn't have long to wait.

'That's the one!' Lizzie cried excitedly, point to one of the panels.

'Great,' said Sam surveying the eight foot tall fence, 'so what do we do now, jump over it or dig a tunnel?'

'Ha ha very funny,' Lizzie replied, 'just watch and all will be revealed.' And with that Lizzie knelt down beside the fence and taking a penknife from a pocket of her denim jacket she set to work on the bolts which secured the corrugated iron panel to a thick wooden post. Forcing the blade of the knife under the rounded head of the lowest bolt, she prized it back until she could get her fingers behind it and then with a tug she pulled it free. Sam watched fascinated as in quick succession three more bolts succumbed to Lizzie's penknife allowing her to pull back a corner of the panel and reveal a glimpse of the scrap yard beyond.

Sam frowned. True he was impressed with the way Lizzie had solved the problem of getting them into the scrap yard but all the same something was not quite right about how she had managed it. Then in a flash it came to him and picking up one of the long bolts which she had removed he held it up in front of Lizzie's face.

'Very impressive but would you care to explain what happened to the nuts?'

'We don't have time to go into that,' snapped Lizzie, 'just follow me and keep quiet.'

And with that she pulled back the panel, squeezed through the opening and disappeared from sight. Not wanting to be left behind, Sam dropped the bolt and followed after her. He found Lizzie waiting for him beside a large high sided van. All its wheels had been removed and in order to keep it off the ground the front and rear axles were propped up on bricks. As he scanned the once impressive sign writing on its panelled side Sam could just make out the word "Removals" and beneath what he took to be the company's name the words "From here to there with care" which he thought quite appropriate given the firm's line of work.

'Come on,' Lizzie whispered, 'and stay close behind me.'

To Lizzie, Vass's scrap yard had long been a special place and although it had been quite a while since she had last paid it a visit, she instinctively knew that once inside she and Sam would be safe. It was her older brother Ted and his two pals, Pete and Archie who had first taken her to what was their secret domain. Well, to be honest they hadn't actually taken her at all; it had been more a case of her tagging along uninvited. Ted had threatened to throw a spanner at her if she didn't go home but she had refused and fearlessly stood her ground with the result that - much to her brother's horror - Pete and Archie had said that if she promised not to cry when she got hurt, she could join the gang.

The scrap yard had been a hive of industry then and although the war had been over for a long time there always seemed to be an endless supply of obsolete military vehicles, tanks, Bren gun carriers and half-track vehicles taking up every inch of space, each waiting its turn to be reduced to scrap metal. The men employed there worked long hours and during the winter nights the glow of acetylene torches could be seen from miles around. But to Ted, Pete, Archie and Lizzie the scrap yard was playground heaven and without giving a thought to the dangers around them, they would scramble over rusting armoured cars and squeeze into the turrets of tanks. The tanks were their favourites of course. Pete would bag the driver's seat and Ted would man the gun, blasting away at make believe enemy vehicles while she and poor old Archie manned the radio and loaded the gun with imaginary shells. It was all great fun. On one occasion though, the yard did prove to be a dangerous place when she fell onto some scrap metal and cut her arm quite badly. Ted had been mortified, not because of her injury but because he knew that their Dad would give him a good hiding for taking her to the yard in the first place. Thankfully – and just before she burst into tears - Pete came to her rescue. Quick as a flash he bandaged the cut with his handkerchief and ruffling her unruly mop of hair, uttered the magic words 'You'll be all right won't you girlie?' And of course she was. She also fell in love with him there and then, as you do when you're an eight year old girl.

Unwittingly, those fun filled days in Vass's scrap yard were to have a profound effect on Pete and her brother Ted for as soon as they were seventeen, the two pals joined the Royal Tank Regiment and a year later they were over in Germany serving with the British Army of the Rhine. Pete wrote to her occasionally and she kept every one of his letters in an empty chocolate box her mum had given her – a gift from Uncle Percy last Christmas. The box also contained a blood soaked handkerchief which she had no intention of ever washing.

The two fugitives left the relative safety of the wheel-less removal van and dodging the numerous potholes full of oily water that pitted the strip of crumbling tarmac which ran the length of the yard; they ran towards a large open fronted lean-to. Once inside, Sam was amazed to see that the entire building was full of doors. Hundreds of them. Car doors, van doors and lorry doors, some without handles, some without glass in their windows, row upon row of them, all stacked together like slices of toast in a giant toast rack.

'This way,' Lizzie hissed, heading for an open doorway at the back of the building.

'Where are we going?' asked Sam, beginning to wish that they had just gone home.

'The engine shed,' Lizzie replied, pointing as she spoke towards a large wooden building at the end of the roadway.

'I see it,' Sam said.

'Okay then, let's go,' said Lizzie as she dashed through the doorway.

The pair had barely covered ten yards when a noise equivalent to a thousand dentists' drills shattered the silence and a blazing shower of sparks fell like a fiery rain onto the roadway in front of them. Terrified, Sam let out a yell. Lizzie however, knowing exactly what was causing the noise and the mini firework display, simply grabbed hold of his arm.

'Come on stupid, it's only old Charlie cutting up some scrap with a grinder.'

Reluctantly, Sam allowed himself to be pulled through the myriad of flying sparks and seconds later the pair found themselves outside the door to the engine shed.

Praying that it wasn't locked, Lizzie turned the door handle and pushed. Thankfully the heavy wooden door swung open.

'Nobody will ever find us in here,' Lizzie said stepping through the doorway. What she didn't know was that had she chanced to look over her shoulder at that precise moment, she would have seen the portly figure of PC Goodrich riding in through the front gates of the scrap yard on his trusty bicycle.

Chapter Three

The One Arm Bandit

O N THE INSIDE the engine shed was not as big as Sam had imagined it would be.

Although he had to admit that from what he could see, it was still pretty impressive and had the four large windows, two at the front and two at the back, not been so encrusted with years of grime and old cobwebs the space within its four walls would have been endowed with a wealth of natural light. As it was, the gloomy interior only served to enhance the air of neglect which hung over the building. Sam looked about for a light switch before deciding that switching on lights might not be such a good idea after all. His attention was then drawn to two enormous benches, constructed from what looked like old railway sleepers, which dominated the room. Suspended above each was a chain operated winch and on each bench there were several huge engine blocks, held in place by massive wooden chocks. Several had already been stripped down, with their cylinder heads and pistons laying beside them. All were covered with rust, as were the discarded spanners, wrenches and crowbars, which lay beside them, with only the copper headed hammers escaping its corrosive embrace.

As Sam wandered between the two benches, he caught sight of a sign on the far wall which read "No Naked Flames". Quite right too he thought, the place reeked of petrol fumes and engine oil, strike a match in here and the whole building would be a blazing inferno in a matter of minutes.

'Come away from there stupid. If one of those falls on …'

'Okay, okay, no need to go into details,' Sam replied, quickly walking away from the benches. 'so what do we do now?'

Lizzie pointed to what appeared to be a small office at the back of the shed.

'We had better wait in there until the coast is clear.'

The room they entered was in fact not an office but the workers' rest room and judging by the thick layer of dust which coated every surface, it like the engine shed, had not been used in a very long time. A small sink with a single tap stood in one corner. Beside it was a worktop with a free-standing gas ring, on top of which sat a large copper kettle. A table stood in the middle of the room with half a dozen chairs clustered around it. A battered sofa and a wall cupboard, home to a collection of mugs, most of which were chipped, completed the inventory.

'Very cosy,' said Sam sarcastically, plonking himself down on the sofa, 'so how long do we have to stay here for?

'I don't know,' said Lizzie, 'why don't tell me you're hungry again?'

It was a well-known fact that Sam liked his food. He could eat for England his mum always said, yet to look at him you wouldn't have guessed it for although he was not exactly skin and bone, nobody could accuse him of being fat. No, the simple truth was that while Sam loved his food – almost any food really – he never seemed to put on any weight. Now his sister Debbie on the other hand… but that's another story.

'No I'm not,' Sam replied, a little put out by the suggestion, 'but if I were,' he said, dipping a hand into his jacket pocket and removing a bar of chocolate, 'like all good boy scouts I've come prepared.'

'But you're not a boy scout are you?' said Lizzie looking very serious.

'Maybe not but you have to admit it's a pretty good motto all the same.'

'I suppose so,' Lizzie said taking a seat on the sofa beside him, 'wasn't there also one about sharing things with your friends?'

Sam smiled, broke the chocolate bar in two and handed half to Lizzie.

After devouring the chocolate bar the two sat in silence, each wrapped up in their own thoughts as to why PC Goodrich was following them.

'Why do you suppose he's following us? You don't think somebody reported us for fishing in Mr Tucker's lake do you Lizzie?'

'No I wouldn't think so, besides Mr Tucker himself has seen us fishing there before and he didn't tell us off did he?'

'No I guess you're right. Bit of a puzzle though don't you think?'

Lizzie frowned. 'Of course it could be that somebody saw you pinching apples from Miss Litchetwood's orchard.'

'I only took two,' admitted Sam ruefully 'and you ate one of them,' he said, reminding Lizzie that she was just as much to blame as him.

Lizzie shrugged her shoulders, 'Oh well maybe he's just keeping an eye on us.'

'What, waiting for us to do something wrong and then pouncing on us?' Well if that's the case,' said Sam, 'we've played right into his hands by breaking into Mr Vass's scrap yard haven't we?'

Lizzie lowered her head. He was right of course. How could she have been so stupid, if PC Goodrich found them here they would really be in big trouble.

Realising that what he had said was a bit tactless, Sam quickly changed the subject. 'So how come nobody works in the engine shed any more then?' he asked.

'Well,' said Lizzie eager to change the topic of conversation, 'it's a pretty sad story really.'

'Go on let's hear it then,' said Sam eager to hear more.

'Well according to my Uncle Percy, Mr Vass's son Vic used to run the engine shed.

He was a real whiz with engines apparently. Anyway like most young men in those days, he was called up to do his National Service and he was sent off to fight in the Korean War. He had only been there for a few months Uncle Percy said when the news came through that Vic had been killed in action. Old Mr Vass was heartbroken and not long afterwards he closed the engine shed down and nobody has ever worked in there since.'

'Blimey,' said Sam, suddenly seeing old Mr Vass and his dilapidated scrap yard in a whole new light, 'poor old Mr Vass.' And with that they both lapsed into silence.

Several minutes passed and then suddenly, right out of the blue Sam asked

'What's that over there?'

'What's what?' Lizzie said taken completely by surprise.

'That,' Sam replied pointing towards a large object in the corner hidden under a sheet of tarpaulin.

'I don't know. I certainly don't remember it being there before.'

'Better check it out then,' said Sam getting up from the sofa and crossing the room.

'I think whatever it is we should just leave it covered up,' Lizzie suggested a little apprehensively.

'Oh come on, it can't hurt to take a look can it?'

'Well okay then,' said Lizzie, curious to see for herself what was hidden under the tarpaulin, 'but be careful and don't break anything.'

Eagerly Sam grabbed a corner of the tarpaulin sheet and pulled. The cover came away effortlessly and fell in a heap onto the floor, revealing as it did so an ancient fruit machine, its chrome and enamelled exterior as bright and shiny as the day it was made.

'Blow me it's a one arm bandit!' Sam cried in amazement.

'So it is,' said Lizzie, equally surprised by what they had discovered, 'whatever is it doing in here?'

'Search me. Maybe the men who worked in the engine shed found it among the scrap and brought it in here for safe keeping.'

'No that can't be right,' Lizzie said looking more than a little puzzled, 'like I said it wasn't in here last time I came and besides which, the engine shed has been shut up for years.'

'Well maybe Mr Vass put it in here. It's probably worth a bob or two I'll bet.'

'Yes but why would he put it in here? It just doesn't make any sense.'

'Well it's here now,' said Sam running his hand over the front of the one arm bandit.

'Hey! maybe it still works, shall we give it a go?'

'No, we had better leave it alone,' said Lizzie, 'besides which, you might break it, you know how accident prone you are.'

But Sam wasn't going to be put off that easily and when he spotted a silver coin lying in the machine's pay out tray, his mind was made up. Grabbing the coin he held it up for Lizzie to see.

'Hey! how lucky is that?' he shouted.

Unconvinced by this apparent good fortune, Lizzie slowly shook her head from side to side.

'No, I still don't think we should touch it.'

'Oh come on Lizzie let's give it a try, you never know we might win the jackpot.'

Despite her reluctance, Lizzie found the urge to see if the one arm bandit still worked too intriguing.

'Oh all right then but if you break it you can take the blame.'

Grinning from ear to ear, Sam stepped up to the machine, pushed the coin into the appropriate slot and grabbing the bandit's "arm" pulled as hard as he could.

Behind the small glass window located at the front of the machine the stylized paintings of fruit; an orange, a bunch of cherries and a lemon all began to rotate, slowly at first then gathering speed until they became a blur. Then quite abruptly; clunk, clunk, clunk each rotating cylinder came to a sudden stop. Stepping up to the machine, Sam and Lizzie peered into the window and as they did so their look of expectation quickly turned to one of puzzlement.

Well they certainly hadn't won the jackpot as not even two pieces of fruit matched. Even more puzzling was the fact that there was no sign of any fruit at all. In fact in the first window where there should have been the picture of an orange there was the figure 21. In the second window where there should have been the picture of a bunch of cherries there was the figure 11 and in the third window instead of a lemon there were the figures 655.

Sam and Lizzie stared at each other in disbelief.

'There, I knew it!' Lizzie exclaimed, 'you've broken it.'

'How could I have done?' Sam replied indignantly, 'all I did was pull the handle down, which incidentally is what you're supposed to do.'

'Well it's broken all the same isn't it? Oh why did I let you touch it?'

'Hey hold on, who says it's broken anyway?'

'Well just take a look,' said Lizzie pointing an accusing finger at the one armed bandit's three windows, 'I don't see any pictures of fruit do you?'

'That's hardly my fault now is it?' said Sam in his own defence.

Lizzie hesitated, he did have a point, I mean why were there numbers instead of pictures of fruit? However, before she had a chance to ponder, she suddenly became aware that the lights, which illuminated the bandit's fascia had begun to flash off and on. Sam noticed them too.

'Perhaps I had better unplug it,' he said a little nervously.

'Yes, good idea,' Lizzie replied, 'then cover it over again.'

Sam peered down behind the fruit machine, looking for the wall socket but there wasn't one. Not only that, but there was no sign of a power cable either.

'Must work off a battery,' Sam said pulling his head out from behind the machine.

Lizzie however didn't appear to hear him, she just stood seemingly mesmerized by the pulsating lights which had now grown much brighter. Sam walked over to her.

'Did you hear what I …' His voice trailed off as he too found his gaze drawn to the flashing lights. Imperceptibly the rhythmical throbbing increased in speed and the light took on a new intensity, becoming brighter and brighter until the whole room was engulfed in a fluorescent glow. As the brilliance of the light intensified an invisible force enveloped the two friends and they found themselves slowly drawn towards the one arm bandit. Instinctively Sam reached out and grabbed hold of Lizzie's arm, calling out to her as he did so, but his words were swallowed up in the vortex of light that now filled the small room. Drawn ever closer towards the one arm bandit, just when it seemed that they would be sucked into the very machine itself, the room suddenly exploded in a star burst of cosmic light.

Chapter Four

Sutton Hoo

SAM AND LIZZIE stared at each other in total disbelief. Instead of being in the rest room of the engine shed they now found themselves standing on a low wooded hillside overlooking the estuary of a large river.

'What..what happened?' Lizzie stuttered, a note of panic in her voice.

'I am not sure,' Sam replied, feeling surprisingly calm about the whole thing. 'The main thing is we seem to be okay. You do feel okay don't you Lizzie?'

Lizzie took a deep breath 'No, since you ask I don't feel okay, I feel scared, really, really scared. I mean how did we get here, wherever here is?'

'I don't know,' said Sam looking around at their unfamiliar surroundings, 'But this is definitely pretty weird.'

An uncomfortable silence followed as they struggled to take in what had happened to them.

'Why aren't we in the scrap yard?' Lizzie asked in a hushed voice.

'I don't really know Lizzie,' replied Sam rubbing his chin thoughtfully. 'but whatever happened to us I've got a sneaky feeling that one arm bandit has got something to do with it.'

'Whatever do you mean?' asked Lizzie frowning.

'Well just think about it for a moment, one minute we are in Mr. Vass's scrap yard playing with an old one arm bandit and the next thing we know we are out here in the middle of who knows where.'

'Yes, but I don't see how playing with that one arm bandit could have anything to do with us being out here,' Lizzie replied looking quite perplexed.

Sam took a moment before answering her. The last thing he wanted was to scare Lizzie but on the other hand he felt he had to tell her what he thought had happened to them even if it did sound completely bonkers.

'Look you're going to think I'm completely mad saying this, but I reckon that one arm bandit was really some kind of time machine.'

Lizzie planted her hands on her hip and stared at him. 'You are joking of course?'

'No I'm not joking, I'm perfectly serious. And before you start laughing, how else do you suppose we...'

'That's just stupid,' said Lizzie cutting Sam off in mid-sentence, 'even I know there's no such thing as time machines and time travel. It's all just a load of rubbish.'

'Well what about Doctor Who and his Tardis then?' said Sam.

'Don't talk silly, Doctor Who is just a television programme, it's not real you know, it's all just made up,' said Lizzie plainly a little annoyed.

Sam shrugged his shoulders. 'Well, ridiculous or not, it's the only explanation I can think of. .. Unless of course we are... .' He let his voice trail off, not wanting to say the D word out loud.

'You don't think we are do you?' asked Lizzie the colour draining from her face.

'What dead?' said Sam finding it quite easy to say the D word after all. 'No definitely not. No this is probably all just a bad dream and we'll wake up in a minute back in Mr. Vass's scrap yard.'

Lizzie stared at the ground, trying to come to terms with what had happened to them and the awful possibility that what Sam had said about the one arm bandit might just be true after all.

'If you're right about that one arm bandit,' Lizzie said 'and I'm not saying I totally believe you, but if it really was a time machine, what was it doing in the engine shed and how did it get there?'

'I don't know,' replied Sam, 'maybe it got there all by itself.'

'What? on the off chance that someone like us would come along?'

'It's possible I suppose,' said Sam, 'I guess time machines can pretty much do whatever they want.' And with that the pair fell silent, each lost in their own thoughts.

'Do you think we are still in England?' Lizzie asked, finally breaking the silence.

'I'm not sure,' said Sam looking around him, 'it looks like England to me and those are definitely oak trees over there.'

Lizzie looked to where Sam was pointing. 'How do you know they're oak trees, they don't have any leaves on them? '

'Because I do,' said Sam, 'I mean anybody can see they're oak trees just by their shape.'

'Okay,' said Lizzie not wanting to argue about it, 'I'll believe you. But don't they have oak trees in other countries too?'

'Maybe they do but they're a different kind of oak tree not like those over there. No they are definitely English oak trees,' said Sam with total conviction.

'So we are in England then?' said Lizzie a little apprehensively.

'Yes I'd say so. Where exactly in England I don't know, but yes I'd say we are definitely in England.'

Although not totally convinced by Sam's knowledge of trees, the thought that they might still be in England after all cheered Lizzie up.

'Well on the off chance we are not in heaven, Lizzie replied sarcastically, 'maybe we should have a look round and try to find out where we are.' Pleased to have the old Lizzie back Sam smiled and pointing to the top of the hill behind them he said.

'Let's go up there, we'll get a better view.'

After a short climb, Sam and Lizzie reached the top of the hill and found themselves confronted by two huge mounds of earth with what appeared to be a deep trench in between them. As soon as she saw the great piles of sandy soil Lizzie felt physically sick. This couldn't be happening she told herself, it's just not possible. But the mounds of earth were real enough and impossible or not, deep down she knew exactly what they were about to discover and it was this which scared her most of all.

Gripping Sam's hand and with her heart pounding, Lizzie walked slowly towards the mounds of earth.

Chapter Five

The Burial Boat

'**B**LIMEY!' CRIED SAM staring down into the deep trench, 'it's a boat. What the heck's a boat doing on the top of a hill?'

Lizzie didn't answer him. She just stood gazing down into the trench, her mind struggling to come to terms with what they had discovered. This just wasn't possible she told herself and yet there it was as large as life, a Viking long-ship.

'Are you okay Lizzie? Only you look like you've just seen a ghost?' said Sam with a hint of concern in his voice.

Lizzie turned towards him 'I know why this boat's here,' she said.

'Oh you do, do you?' said Sam.

'Yes,' said Lizzie confidently, 'I also know where we are.'

'Oh and where exactly are we then clever clogs?'

'We are at a place called Sutton Hoo.'

'Sutton what?' said Sam a puzzled look on his face.

'Sutton Hoo. It's in Suffolk,' said Lizzie hardly daring to believe what she had just said.

'Suffolk!' Sam exclaimed. 'Oh well at least I was right about us being in England then.'

'Oh we are in England alright,' said Lizzie, 'that's the good news anyway.'

'So what's the bad news then?' said Sam a little surprised by Lizzie's last comment.

'The bad news is that it's not 1965.'

'How on earth do you know that?'

'Because of that,' said Lizzie pointing at the boat.

'I don't get it,' said Sam looking thoroughly confused, 'just because we've found some old boat you're telling me it's not 1965.'

'Yes' said Lizzie in a firm voice.

'And how come you're so sure that we are in this place called Sutton Hoo?'

'Because it's where they found that boat.'

'You've completely lost me now,' Sam said shaking his head.

Lizzie frowned. This wasn't going to be easy. 'Look before I tell you anymore about that boat and why it's here, I think it's best if you sit down.'

'What, so now you're going to give me a history lesson are you?' said Sam.

'Sort of. But I still think you should sit down,' said Lizzie a serious tone to her voice.

'I'll stand if you don't mind,' Sam replied, folding his arms across his chest, 'just keep it brief will you I have a short attention span remember.'

'Okay but don't say I didn't warn you.'

'Just get on with it Lizzie …Please!'

'Right,' said Lizzie composing herself 'At the start of last term I joined Mr Horne's history club, we meet after school every Monday…'

'I didn't know that,' interrupted Sam, 'I didn't think girls liked history.'

'Well it just so happens that I do,' said Lizzie 'now if you'll just let me finish! The Monday before last Mr Horne was telling us about the early Anglo Saxon kings of East Anglia and in particular about a Royal family called Wuffing. With me so far?'

'With you,' said Sam trying not to sound bored.

'Okay then, now this is where it gets a bit weird…You sure you don't want to sit down?'

Sam scowled but said nothing.

'Well anyway,' continued Lizzie, 'according to Mr Horne it's a proven fact that the Wuffing Royal family were buried at a place called Sutton Hoo.'

'How come they know that for sure?' inquired Sam, suddenly taking an interest.

'Because the Wuffings had a royal hall at Rendlesham which is just a few miles away from Sutton Hoo and besides which there were sixteen other burial mounds here too.'

'What, you mean there are sixteen more boats buried up here?' inquired Sam looking around the hill top.

'No just this one as far as anyone knows,' said Lizzie, 'anyway let me finish or you're only going to get confused.'

'Okay carry on,' said Sam suddenly a little more interested in what Lizzie had to say.

'Well in 1939 a man called Brown excavated the biggest of the mounds and found a boat, well not an actual boat, just the remains of one.'

'And you're saying that this,' said Sam pointing a finger at the boat 'is the boat he found?'

'Yes,' Lizzie replied as calmly as she could.

Sam's face suddenly went a deathly white and he sat down on the ground with a bump.

'Are you alright?' said Lizzie, a worried note in her voice.

Sam didn't answer. He just stared down at the boat, dumbstruck.

'I did warn you it would be a bit of a shock,' said Lizzie 'and I know it's hard to believe but there's just no other explanation. This has to be the very same boat, which he found in 1939.'

Sam continued to stare at the boat. This was all getting a little too weird for his liking. I mean it was bad enough finding themselves out in the countryside miles from Tingwick without it being 1939 for goodness sake. And then he had a Eureka moment.

'I know what it is,' he cried excitedly, 'it's a replica; they've built a replica boat and put it where this Mr Brown found the old one.'

Lizzie smiled. 'Nice try but not true I'm afraid.'

'How do you know that?' said Sam jumping to his feet.

'Because if there had been a replica of the boat then Mr Horne would have told us about it. I mean he actually came to Sutton Hoo a little while ago, that's why he was telling us all about it at History club. So it stands to reason that if there had been a replica I'm pretty sure he would have mentioned it don't you? Besides, he took some photos while he was here so I'm pretty sure that if this 'replica' had been here he would have taken a picture of it.'

'Yes,' shouted Sam, walking over to one of the mounds, 'but just look at the soil, I'd say this trench has only just been dug wouldn't you? So maybe it wasn't here when Mr Horne came.'

'It's possible I suppose,' said Lizzie a little uncertainly.

'Well there you are then, mystery solved,' said Sam beaming, 'so now all we have to do is find a way of getting from Sutton Hoo back to Tingwick. Do you have any money on you?'

'Why?' said Lizzie a little puzzled by the question.

'For the bus fare of course, I mean they must have a bus service even out here.'

Lizzie shrugged her shoulders and looked down at the boat. In her heart she knew Sam was mistaken. This was no replica, this was the very same boat that had been unearthed in 1939. The only difference was that the boat she was looking at right now hadn't even been buried yet!

'Sam,' said Lizzie changing the subject, 'do you remember what the numbers were that came up on the one arm bandit?'

'What, instead of the fruit you mean?'

'Yes.'

'Err, let me see now… The first one was twenty one and I think the second was eleven. I don't remember what the third number was.'

'The third number was six hundred and fifty five,' said Lizzie.

'If you say so,' said Sam a little puzzled as to why Lizzie was so interested in the numbers anyway.'

'Well, I'm pretty sure it's meant to be a date,' said Lizzie.

'How come?' asked Sam.

'Well if you read from left to right you get the twenty first of the eleventh six hundred and fifty five,' said Lizzie.

'That's not right,' said Sam 'I mean six hundred and fifty five isn't even a proper year.

A year has to have four figures right?'

'Not if it's AD,' Lizzie replied in a hushed voice.

'AD' mimicked Sam, what's AD?'

'It stands for Anno Domini. The year of our Lord.'

'So?' said Sam looking even more puzzled.

'So, six hundred and fifty five AD is a year and what's more,' said Lizzie pointing at the long boat, 'it's the same year that this boat was buried!'

Sam's mouth fell open and despite his legs turning to jelly he somehow managed to remain standing.

'Remember I said that Sutton Hoo was a burial site for the Wuffing royal family?'

Still in shock, Sam could only nod his head.

'Well one of their kings was buried in this boat.'

'What, they used a boat as a coffin?' said Sam regaining his voice.

'Yes and this is the very boat that they used to bury him in.'

'I'm sorry,' Sam said totally perplexed by the whole thing, 'you've lost me.'

'Well,' Lizzie continued 'when Mr Brown discovered the burial boat he also found a load of treasure including a fantastic gold and silver helmet and that's how they knew when the boat had been buried.'

'So which king was buried here then?' asked Sam suddenly becoming interested in hearing more.

'No one knows,' said Lizzie, 'because they never found a body.'

'What, they buried a ship full of treasure but forgot to bury the king with it?'

'No, according to Mr Horne most historians believe that a king was buried here, they just can't agree on which one that's all. Most think it was a king called Raedwald but nobody really knows for sure.'

'Crikey!' cried Sam, with a wild look in his eyes, 'so I was right then?'

'Right about what?' said Lizzie frowning.

'About that one arm bandit being a time machine of course,' said Sam excitedly.

'Well I don't see why you should feel so pleased with yourself,' Lizzie replied, tears welling up in her eyes. 'I mean what if we are stuck here for the rest of….

'Hey don't worry,' said Sam placing his arm around Lizzie's shoulder, 'things will work out you'll see.'

Comforted by Sam's gesture, Lizzie looked up at him and smiled bravely.

'That's better,' Sam said, quite relieved that Lizzie hadn't actually burst into tears.

'Anyway at least we know where we are now and if you're right about the date we even know what year it is.'

'Oh and that's supposed to help us is it?' said Lizzie dabbing at her nose with the sleeve of her jacket.

'Well no, I don't suppose so, but at least we know how the time machine works' said

Sam. 'And besides.'

'Besides what?' asked Lizzie composing herself.

'Well don't you see, this is going to be the best adventure ever,' enthused Sam.

Despite her reservations Lizzie found herself smiling at Sam's sense of optimism. 'I suppose you're right,' she said, 'at least there's no point in worrying about things I guess.'

'That's the spirit,' said Sam grinning from ear to ear. 'Never say die as my old Uncle Herbert used to say.'

The two young friends stared at each other for what seemed to be an age. Incredibly, thanks to discovering that one arm bandit they had been transported back in time to the year 655 AD, to an ancient barrow cemetery where a royal boat burial was about to take place. A boat, which would lie undisturbed, for one thousand three hundred and ten years until its discovery in 1939.

'Well since we are here,' said Sam breaking the silence, 'why don't we take a look at the boat, I mean you never know we might even get to see that treasure you mentioned.'

'Good idea,' said Lizzie suddenly quite keen to be doing something and she followed Sam as he stepped onto a wide wooden plank which acted as a bridge onto the curved prow of the boat.

The boat itself was built of timber and was at least twenty seven meters long and almost four and a half meters across at its widest point. Rows of narrow benches for oarsmen to sit on spanned the hull at regular intervals and down the centre a narrow walkway ran from bow to stern. There was no sign of a mast or a sail but where the mast should have been was a curious cabin constructed of wooden panels and a sloping wooden roof.

'Do you think that that's where they would have put the dead king?' said Sam pointing towards the cabin, 'seems likely,' Lizzie replied.

'Perhaps he's in there now.'

'I hope not,' said Lizzie taking a step back.

'Well the least we can do is take a look don't you think, just to make sure?'

'No I don't think that's a very good idea,' replied Lizzie a touch of panic in her voice.

'Look what happened the last time your curiosity got the better of you.'

'Well, I am going to have a look anyway,' said Sam choosing to ignore Lizzie's comment.

'I can't see that just taking a look will do any harm.' And with that he disappeared inside the wooden cabin.

Lizzie waited anxiously as the minutes ticked by. Finally, after what seemed like an age, Sam reappeared. 'Empty, no dead king, no treasure, just some old pots and pans,' he said obviously disappointed.

'Thank goodness for that,' said Lizzie quite relieved, 'now I think we should leave.'

'And go where?' asked Sam

Before she could reply Lizzie found herself distracted by something. 'Did you hear that?'

'Hear what?' said Sam.

'That noise. It's a long way off but it sounds a bit like people's voices.'

'I can't hear a ... Wait a minute, now I can hear it,' shouted Sam.

'I think it's coming from down there,' cried Lizzie pointing towards the river.

'Come on then,' shouted Sam, 'let's go and check it out.'

Retracing their steps across the plank Sam and Lizzie ran to where they could get a view of the river.

Reaching the brow of the hill they both stopped dead in their tracks and stared in utter disbelief at what they saw.

Chapter Six

Invisible

BELOW THEM OUT in the estuary, two long-ships, their brightly coloured sails swollen by a stiff breeze blowing in from the sea, were heading straight for the shore, the rhythmic chanting from the crews as they dipped their oars into the choppy waters, growing louder with each stroke. Sam was the first to react.

'Come on,' he said, 'we have to hide.'

And grabbing Lizzie's hand he began running toward the woods on the far side of the hill.

Reluctantly Lizzie allowed him to lead her away.

'Oh Sam isn't it just fantastic?' cried Lizzie excitedly.

'I can think of another word for it,' said Sam dragging Lizzie along behind him 'it begins with S and rhymes with hairy.'

Lizzie threw a look over her shoulder but didn't reply.

'Come on Lizzie we can hide in those trees over there.'

'But they are coming ashore;' Lizzie shouted 'shouldn't we at least go and speak to them?'

'Err, no I don't think that's such a good idea,' said Sam yanking on Lizzie's arm 'they don't look very friendly to me.'

A minute later, a very relieved Sam dragged Lizzie into the cover of the trees and pulled her down onto the ground beside him.

'You don't think they saw us do you?' said Sam slightly out of breath.

'No I shouldn't think so. I think we were too far away.'

'Phew! that's a relief.'

'Well,' said Lizzie catching her breath, 'I guess this makes what I said about the burial boat true doesn't it?'

'I'm glad you're taking all this so calmly,' said Sam 'I mean this is pretty scary stuff you know.'

'Did you make out what they were shouting?' asked Lizzie caught up in what was happening and not feeling in the least bit frightened.

'Blimey you're a cool customer,' said Sam 'you do realize don't you that if you're right about that boat, then you know who those people are don't you?'

'Course I do silly!' said Lizzie her face flushed with excitement.

'And have you thought what they might do to us if they catch us?'

Lizzie didn't answer. Sam was right of course, here she was treating it all like some sort of game when in fact they could both be in real danger. 'I guess you're right,' Lizzie said a little reluctantly.

'Of course I'm right,' said Sam, 'anyway for now we just watch and see what happens, agreed?'

'Agreed,' said Lizzie a smile spreading across her face as she spotted some acorns lying on the ground. At least Sam had been right about the trees she thought to herself.

The minutes ticked by and as the two long-ships drew closer to the shore, the cries of the oarsmen carried up to where Sam and Lizzie were hiding.

'Can you make out what they are saying?'

'Not sure,' said Sam straining his ears, 'sounds like over here or something.'

'Maybe it's not overhere,' cried Lizzie excitedly, 'maybe what they are shouting is Aethelhere!'

'Oh and who's Aethelhere when he's at home then?'

Well according to Mr Horne, there are some historians who think he could be the king who was buried here.'

'Now I am confused,' said Sam 'I thought you said a king called Raedwald was buried here?'

'Well to begin with that's what most historians thought, but then later on when they were able to date the coins which were found among the treasure more accurately, they discovered that he had died over twenty years before the burial.'

'In that case it's not likely to have been him then is it?'

'No very unlikely,' said Lizzie smiling at his apparent interest.

'Okay so how come they think it was this chap Aethelhere then?'

'Well he was a king from the Royal house of Wuffing too and the date of his death ties in with the date of the burial.'

'Go on,' said Sam

'Well according to the history book Mr Horne read to us, in November six hundred and fifty five Aethelhere and a king called Penda were both killed fighting against the Northumbrians.'

'So it could be this King Penda who is buried here then and not Aethelhere?'

'No,' said Lizzie, 'he was a Mercian King not an Anglo Saxon one.'

'This is getting complicated,' said Sam shaking his head despairingly.

'It's really quite simple,' said Lizzie 'Mercia was the ancient name for the Midlands so there's no way Penda would have been buried here in East Anglia.'

Sam pulled a face but said nothing.

'Anyway,' Lizzie continued ignoring Sam's pained expression, 'according to historical accounts the battle was fought beside a flooded river and lots of Penda's and Aethelhere's soldiers were drowned during the battle and their bodies washed away.'

'Oh and that's why these historians think the reason why they didn't find a body in the boat was because it was lost in a river?'

'Correct!'

Sam mulled this over for a few moments. 'Bit careless wasn't it?' he said finally.

'What do you mean?' said Lizzie.

'Well, first they let their King get killed, which is bad enough but then they go and lose his body as well.'

'I don't suppose they did it on purpose,' said Lizzie rolling her eyes in exasperation, 'anyway who said they did lose it, maybe the king's body is on one of those ships we've just seen.'

'What!' said Sam sitting bolt upright, 'you're joking right?'

'Well I can't think of any other reason for them being here can you?'

'Blimey! So you really think they've come here to bury this King Aethelhere?'

'Yes,' said Lizzie, 'I mean it all makes perfect sense, 'we've seen the burial boat right? And now these two ships arrive. Well it can't just be a coincidence can it?'

'Flipping heck!' exclaimed Sam, 'this is all getting a bit surreal don't you think?'

'I guess so,' said Lizzie, 'but don't you see how it all fits into place?'

'If you say so,' said Sam totally bemused by everything.

Cheer up' said Lizzie smiling, 'after all you were right about one thing.'

'Oh and what's that?' inquired Sam.

'We really have travelled back in time.'

Before either of them could say another word on the subject, a rabbit suddenly appeared from beneath a nearby bush and came hopping towards them.

Sam's immediate reaction was to reach for a short piece of branch which lay on the ground next to him.

'Don't you dare,' hissed Lizzie knowing exactly what Sam had in mind.

Apparently unaware of their presence the rabbit hopped closer.

'But we have to eat,' whispered Sam, his hand closing around the branch.

'You've just had a bar of chocolate remember?' said Lizzie as loud as she dare.

'Half a bar actually,' said Sam 'and that was ages ago.'

Another couple of hops and the rabbit was in range of Sam's club but just as he raised the length of branch above his head, Lizzie suddenly clapped her hands together and shouted out 'Shoo! Shoo!'

Sam was so surprised that he almost dropped the branch. But what was even more surprising was that the rabbit didn't even blink an eye.

'Now that's very odd,' said Sam, slowly lowering the branch. 'Either it's deaf and blind or that's one very brave bunny rabbit.'

'I see what you mean,' said Lizzie studying the rabbit as it carried on nibbling the grass quite unconcerned.

'Perhaps it's got Myxomatosis?' said Sam.

'No I don't think so, its eyes aren't all red and swollen. Besides, I don't think rabbits caught Myxomatosis in the old days' said Lizzie more than a little puzzled by the rabbit's behaviour.

'Well why didn't it run off then?' said Sam dropping the length of branch onto the ground.

'Because,' said Lizzie the answer suddenly dawning on her, 'it doesn't know we are here.' To demonstrate the point, Lizzie got to her feet and slowly walked towards the rabbit. As she drew closer the rabbit stopped feeding and pricked up its ears. Lizzie froze. A moment later apparently satisfied that it was in no immediate danger the rabbit went back to its meal. Cautiously, Lizzie inched forward until she was within touching distance of the animal. Instantly the rabbit's head came up. 'Well it definitely can't see me but I think it can sense that I'm here,' said Lizzie.

By way of confirmation no sooner had she spoken than the rabbit hopped away and with a bob of its tail, it disappeared into the bush it had emerged from previously.

'Wow!' exclaimed Sam, 'you know what this means don't you? We're invisible!'

While Sam hadn't expected Lizzie to jump with joy at the prospect of being invisible, he hadn't expected her to just stand still and say nothing either. But before he could say anything, with a look of amazement on her face, Lizzie suddenly flung out her arm and pointing at something over Sam's shoulder she cried out.

'Sam look they're here!'

Sam swung around and instantly saw what Lizzie was pointing at, or to be more precise, who she was pointing at.

'Jeepers so they are,' said Sam, staring wide eyed at the two lines of Saxon Warriors striding up the hillside towards them, the late afternoon sun glinting on their helmets.

'Quick get down.' he shouted and instinctively they both dropped to their knees.

'They must have seen us after all,' whispered Sam, 'and now they've come looking for us.'

'Don't be silly they're not looking for us,' said Lizzie smiling, 'they have come to bury their king remember?'

'I hope you're right,' said Sam 'because they look a pretty mean bunch to me.'

Lizzie didn't bother to reply, she was far more interested in watching the two ranks of Saxon warriors as they marched closer to their hiding place.

There were at least forty warriors in each file; tall men with bearded faces, their long hair tied in braids and a cloak thrown over their broad shoulders. Every one of them carried a spear and shield with a sword hanging from a belt at their waist. Leading them was a standard bearer, a richly embroidered banner held high above his head for all to see. At the centre of the procession and flanked by the two ranks of Saxon warriors were four men carrying a litter and resting on it was a simple wooden coffin, its carved lid held in place by heavy iron fittings.

'Look Sam,' cried Lizzie excitedly, 'do you see those four men? They're carrying a coffin.'

'So I see,' Sam replied without too much enthusiasm.

'You know what this means don't you?'

'What! that you're right again?' said Sam clearly a bit miffed.

'Yes,' said Lizzie, 'but that's not what I meant.'

'So what did you mean then clever clogs?'

'What I meant was that as there's a coffin it must mean that a body was buried in the boat after all and if those men were chanting Aethelhere, then it has to be his.'

'Course the coffin could be empty, had you thought of that?' said Sam.

'Oh and it takes four strong men to carry an empty coffin does it?' replied Lizzie a hint of sarcasm in her voice.

'You're probably right,' said Sam shrugging his shoulders. 'Well I guess there's only one way to find out for sure.' And with that he turned and walked away.

'Where are you going?' cried Lizzie.

'I'm going to take a closer look,' said Sam matter of factly.

'Are you mad?' said Lizzie.

'Look, just stay put and I'll be back before you know it,' said Sam calmly.

'But what if they see you?' asked Lizzie, horrified at what Sam planned to do.

'Haven't you forgotten something?' he said.

'What's that?' asked Lizzie.

'I'm invisible remember?'

Chapter Seven

Aethelhere

SAM WALKED OUT from the wood and began running as fast as he could across the open ground. As he drew nearer to the lines of Saxon warriors he was immediately struck by just how fierce and powerful they looked, which led him to think that what he was doing was probably not such a good idea after all. But it was too late to turn back now, besides which, he was in full view so if they were going to see him, there was not a thing he could do about it. Strangely though not a single head turned in his direction and not one warrior broke ranks to challenge him. He could almost reach out and touch them and yet the ranks of Saxon warriors filed past as if he wasn't there.

Lizzie watched in horror as Sam ran across the stretch of open ground and made a beeline for the front of the burial precession which by now was less than thirty meters away from where she was hiding. Surely any minute now and they are bound to see him she thought to herself and then what? But to her total amazement as Sam drew closer to the ranks of Saxon warriors not a single one of them so much as glanced in his direction. After a moment's hesitation, she took a deep breath, stepped out from the trees and ran as fast as her legs would carry her across the grassy hillside towards Sam. Seconds later and a little out of breath and she was standing beside him staring in amazement at the ranks of Saxon warriors filing past them.

'It's just like it was with the rabbit Lizzie,' shouted Sam excitedly. 'They can't see us!'

Just as she was about to reply, Lizzie saw the Saxon warrior nearest to them quickly turn his head and look in their direction. Instantly she grabbed Sam's arm and pulled him away.

'Shush,' she whispered, 'did you see that, he looked right at us?'

'Yes,' said Sam, 'but he didn't see us did he?'

'I know,' hissed Lizzie, 'but something spooked him.'

'Maybe we just got too close,' said Sam trying not to make too much of it.

'I don't think it's just that,' said Lizzie.

'What you mean he heard what I said?'

'No not exactly… It's hard to explain really but it's like although he couldn't see us, as soon as you spoke he somehow sensed we were there.'

'All seems a bit weird if you ask me,' said Sam, 'maybe we're in some parallel universe or something.'

'What ever do you mean?' asked Lizzie puzzled by Sam's statement.

'Well,' said Sam sounding quite serious, 'my Dad took me to the pictures on my last birthday and we saw this film about a space ship, which crashed on a strange planet.

Anyway, it seems that as well as travelling through space, without knowing it the people on the space ship had also travelled through time.'

'Meaning what exactly?' said Lizzie beginning to get a little exasperated.

'Meaning,' said Sam, 'that because they had come from another time, the people on the planet didn't know they were there. It was like they were standing behind a one way mirror; they could see out but nobody could see in.'

'Well I still don't get it?' said Lizzie pointing at the ranks of Saxon warriors, 'surely if we can see them, then it stands to reason they should be able to see us doesn't it?'

'Well they can't and that's that,' said Sam becoming exasperated, 'so let's stop worrying about it okay?'

'I guess you're right, 'Lizzie replied 'but....'

'Look,' interrupted Sam, 'let's just say the reason why nobody can see us is because we're not supposed to be here and leave it at that.'

'Oh all right then,' said Lizzie reluctantly, 'but just to be on the safe side we don't get too close to them and we keep our voices down when we speak. Agreed?'

'Fine by me,' said Sam with a customary shrug of the shoulders.

At that very moment the four coffin bearers appeared. Grim faced they trudged up the grassy incline the weight of the litter and coffin bearing down heavily on their shoulders. Following a few paces behind them was an elderly man wearing a rich purple robe embroidered with gold, and held at the waist by a wide leather belt fastened with a silver buckle. In one hand he carried a long sword, its exquisitely engraved blade resting on his shoulder. In the other, he held a fearsome looking battle axe, its polished head glinting in the last rays of sunshine. Walking beside him, also dressed in a purple robe, was a young boy of about Sam's age.

Gripped tightly in the boy's hands was a huge circular shield, its embossed surface decorated with pagan symbols beautifully crafted in gold and silver. Bringing up the rear of the procession were two warriors carrying a large wooden chest.

'Who do you suppose the boy is?' whispered Sam.

'I don't know,' said Lizzie following the young Saxon with her eyes as he walked past her.

'Do you suppose he could be the dead king's son?' asked Sam.

'I guess he could be,' Lizzie replied. 'I think Mr Horne did say that King Aethelhere had a son but I can't be sure.'

'Well he looks pretty regal to me,' said Sam, 'and maybe that's the king's shield he's carrying, what do you think?'

'It has to be, I remember it from the pictures Mr Horne showed us of the treasure they found in the burial boat.'

'Wow, how cool is that!'

As the last of the Saxon warriors strode past them Sam and Lizzie looked at each other.

'What do we do now?' asked Lizzie.

'I say we follow them,' said Sam. And when Lizzie didn't reply, 'be a shame not to see the actual burial don't you think?'

Lizzie smiled and nodded. Sam was right of course, given everything that had happened to them it somehow seemed only fitting that they go and see the king's burial for themselves.

By the time Sam and Lizzie reached the burial site the two ranks of Saxon warriors had already positioned themselves in a long line down both sides of the wide trench.

'Let's go up there,' whispered Sam pointing towards the mound of earth nearest to them.

'Good idea,' said Lizzie and together they clambered to the top of the slope.

'There,' said Sam when they reached the top, 'ringside seats!'

As Sam and Lizzie gazed down from their vantage point, two of the coffin bearers lifted the oak coffin from the litter and accompanied by the royal standard bearer, they made their way onto the boat. As they did so, the ranks of watching Saxon warriors lowered their heads in respect as the two pallbearers carried the dead king to his final resting place inside the wooden chamber. Moments later the three men emerged again and slowly made their way back across the gang plank.

'Now what happens?' whispered Sam. But before Lizzie could answer him, the elderly man and the young boy, followed by the two men carrying the heavy chest, began making their way across the gang plank.

'That's the king's treasure,' said Lizzie in a low voice.

'What you mean the treasure this Mr Brown found?'

'Yes,' said Lizzie in a hushed voice.

'Blimey,' whispered Sam, 'and nobody is going to see it again for err…'

'For one thousand three hundred and ten years,' said Lizzie after doing a quick calculation in her head...

'That's unbelievable,' said Sam.

'Unbelievable is right' replied Lizzie smiling.

'Wish we could have got a look at it,' said Sam ruefully.

'Well we can't and that's all there is to it,' said Lizzie.

'We could just go down and take a look,' said Sam, 'after all we are invisible remember?'

'No way!' snapped Lizzie quite alarmed by Sam's suggestion. 'It's too dangerous.'

'But what if…'

'No!' said Lizzie before Sam could finish, 'and that's final!'

Sam shrugged his shoulders. He knew when he was beaten.

Having placed the chest inside the burial chamber the two men then left the boat and joined the line of warriors watching in silence as their king was laid to rest. Minutes ticked by until finally the elderly man and young boy emerged empty handed from the burial chamber and with heads bowed, made their way off the boat.

With the burial ship now empty except for the body of the dead king, a great silence hung in the air. Over to the west the setting sun began to dip below the horizon, the last of its rays striking the shields of the motionless ranks of Saxon warriors like golden arrows. As Sam and Lizzie watched spellbound, a tall warrior dressed in a blue cloak stepped forward and drawing his sword from its scabbard he held it aloft.

Instantly a great cry went up from the watching ranks of Saxon warriors.

'Aethelhere, Aethelhere, Aethelhere…' Three times they cried out the dead king's name and then fell silent. Sheathing his sword, the tall warrior pulled his cloak across his chest and in a loud voice he shouted out a command and immediately every warrior began scooping up the sandy soil from the mounds behind them with their shields and throwing it down onto the boat. The burial had begun.

As they stared in total amazement at the scene below them Sam and Lizzie suddenly became aware that their view of the burial boat and the rows of Saxon warriors was becoming distorted. It was almost as though they were looking though a shimmering heat haze.

'What's happening?' cried Lizzie in alarm.

'I don't know,' said Sam a note of concern in his voice.

But before either of them could utter another word, they were enveloped in an inky darkness and the last thing Sam remembered was reaching out and taking hold of Lizzie's hand.

Chapter Eight

Apprehended

SAM AND LIZZIE stood and stared at each other. Had it all been a dream? I mean, here they were in the rest room of the engine shed and yet a moment ago they had been watching an Anglo Saxon boat burial taking place at somewhere called Sutton Hoo.

'Err this may seem like a stupid question,' said Sam hesitantly, 'but did we just go back in time and see some king called Aethelhere being buried in a boat?'

'Yes I think we did,' replied Lizzie hardly daring to believe what she had just said.

'No that can't be right,' said Sam, 'perhaps we just fell asleep.'

'What and we both had the same dream?' said Lizzie looking across the room at the one arm bandit standing just as they had found it in the corner of the room. 'You do remember what happened when you played that machine don't you?'

'Course I do,' said Sam remembering the numbers appearing in the windows instead of the fruit and the explosion of light which had engulfed them.

'I wonder if the numbers are still there,' said Lizzie excitedly, 'if they are it will prove that it wasn't a dream after all.'

Quick as a flash they both crossed the room and looked into the glass window.

'Fruit!' said Sam disappointingly, 'just pictures of fruit.'

'Yes but there were numbers, remember?' said Lizzie.

'I don't know what to think,' said Sam dejectedly, 'I mean how do we really know we went back in time to this Sutton Hoo place?'

'Because I know we did,' said Lizzie, her face suddenly lighting up with a broad smile.

'Oh and you can prove it can you?' asked Sam.

'As a matter of fact I can,' said Lizzie triumphantly. And with that she put a hand into her jacket pocket and pulled out a handful of acorns.

'You do remember the oak trees don't you?'

For a moment Sam was dumbstruck.

'Blimey Lizzie how awesome is that. So it's true we really did go back in time then?'

Before Lizzie could answer him, the door to the rest room suddenly burst open and PC Goodrich, ducking to avoid hitting his helmet on the door frame, entered the room.

'So this is your little hiding place is it? Thought you could out fox me did you? Well let me tell you it takes more than a couple of apple scrumping kids to…' Then quite unexpectedly PC Goodrich stopped in mid-sentence and stared at the one arm bandit.

'Well blow me down it's a Watling Rol-A-Top!' he exclaimed, 'and what a beauty it is too.'

Now, how you might ask, did a police constable from a sleepy Bedfordshire village come to know so much about one arm bandits? Well I don't think it will be giving too much away if I tell you that as a young officer in the Metropolitan Police he was once fortunate enough to visit North America and leave it at that.

'Don't see many of these around you know,' he said more to himself than to the two surprised children. 'Does it still work?'

And before Sam or Lizzie could answer him PC Goodrich reached out and grabbed hold of the handle.

'No harm in giving it a try I suppose.'

Terrified, Sam leaped forward.

'No don't pull….'

But it was too late, the handle had already completed its downward journey and as Sam and Lizzie watched in horror, the three rows of fruit slowly began to rotate.

'Oh no,' groaned Sam reaching out and taking hold of Lizzie's hand, 'here we go again.'

Chapter Nine

Montana

THEY DIDN'T SO much land with a bump, as just suddenly find themselves standing in a vast field of grass. Grass as high as an elephant's eyes, well as high as Sam's waist anyway, an ocean of it, stretching out in every direction for as far as you could see. Scorched by the sun it rippled in the breeze as though an invisible hand were brushing over it. After looking around for what seemed like ages in stunned silence, it was Lizzie who spoke first and all she could say was.

'Amazing!'

'True,' said Sam quick to point out the obvious, 'but more to the point, where are we this time?'

'Don't know,' Lizzie replied 'but it's definitely not Sutton Hoo, that's for sure.'

'Did you get a look at the date?' asked Sam hopefully. Before she could reply, PC Goodrich suddenly let out a loud groan and slumped down onto the ground, his more than generous backside cushioning his landing.

'He doesn't look too good,' said Sam staring into the policeman's face, which had turned a rather pasty white colour, 'probably in shock.'

'Of course he's in shock, stupid,' said Lizzie reaching down and removing PC Goodrich's helmet and placing it on the ground. 'Well don't just stand there, undo his top button or something.'

But before Sam had a chance to comply with Lizzie's suggestion, PC Goodrich sat bolt upright.

'Top buttons to remain fastened,' he said reaching out for his helmet and placing it on his balding head, 'and helmets to be worn at all times.'

Sam and Lizzie looked at each other and then back at PC Goodrich whose face now appeared to have a little more colour.

'Well grab hold then,' said the constable stretching out his arms, 'and help me up.'

Sam and Lizzie each took hold of an arm and pulled. At first nothing happened with PC Goodrich remaining rooted to the spot.

'Put your backs into it!' exclaimed PC Goodrich.

Sam and Lizzie both took a deep breath and digging their heels into the ground, they tried again and slowly but surely they hauled the portly policeman onto his feet.

'How do you feel?' enquired Lizzie.

'Fine! Just fine,' PC Goodrich replied brushing some strands of grass from his uniform jacket, 'just felt a little queasy for a moment that's all. Nothing to worry about.'

'I suppose it must have been a bit of a shock for you constable,' said Sam in a concerned voice, 'I mean it's not every day you get to travel back in time is it?'

For a moment the two friends thought PC Goodrich was going to fall over again but to his credit he managed to remain upright.

'Time travel!' exclaimed PC Goodrich quickly regaining his composure, 'what ever are you talking about?'

'Sounds pretty weird doesn't it?' said Sam breaking into a smile, 'but that's what's happened.'

'Preposterous!' cried PC Goodrich going red in the face, 'I've never heard anything so ridiculous in my life.'

Lizzie stepped forward and took hold of PC Goodrich's hand.

Perhaps you should sit down again while we explain things to you.'

PC Goodrich was about to remonstrate, but upon seeing the concerned expression on Lizzie's face, he changed his mind and sat back down on the ground.

Kneeling down beside him, Lizzie placed a hand on PC Goodrich's shoulder.

'I know it sounds strange, impossible even but if you'll just let me explain.' Seeing that PC Goodrich wasn't going to object, Lizzie removed her hand and went on. 'That machine, that one arm bandit, the Watling Rol …. whatever, which you seem to know so much about, well it isn't a one arm bandit at all, it's some kind of time machine.'

With a snort of derision PC Goodrich blurted out.

'But that's...'

In a firm voice Lizzie cut him short.

'Please just let me finish.'

Sensing that any further remonstration was useless, PC Goodrich let out a sigh and gave a slight nod of his head.

Taking a deep breath Lizzie continued. 'All I,' then she paused and looked across at Sam. 'All we know is that when we pulled the handle on that thing we ended up in Sutton Hoo and watched a Saxon King being buried.'

Sensing a further interruption from PC Goodrich she instinctively held up her hand

'Yes I know it sounds unbelievable but it's true, you have to believe me.'

Sadly, even though he didn't say anything, it was clear from the condescending look, which he gave Lizzie, that PC Goodrich was in fact totally unconvinced by her attempted explanation.

Right thought Sam, deciding it was time that he took matters in hand. Shock tactics are what's needed to wipe that smug look off his face he thought and bending down, with a frown forming a deep crease between his eyebrows, he enquired in a rather condescending tone of voice.

'Where do you reckon we are then constable? Only,' making a sweeping gesture with his arm, 'only this doesn't look at all like Bedfordshire to me, does it to you?'

Sensing that his bluff had been called, PC Goodrich knew that he had no alternative other than to admit to the possibility that they were indeed somewhere other than where they had been when he had pulled the handle on that damn machine.

Resolved to get to the bottom of things, without a word PC Goodrich clambered unaided to his feet and shielding his eyes against the fierce glare of the sun, he looked around him, slowly turning in a full three hundred and sixty degree circle.

'Well?', asked Sam, cocking his head to one side and folding his arms across his chest, mimicking the posture his mother adopted whenever his Dad was late back from the pub and his supper had gone cold. 'Any idea where we are then constable?'

PC Goodrich remained silent, his gaze still fixed on the horizon. Well the cheeky little so and so was right about one thing, they were most definitely not in Bedfordshire, in fact he was pretty sure that they weren't even in England. Then suddenly it dawned on him, ridiculous as it seemed, he began to realise that he had been here before. In fact the more he thought about it the more sure he was. He had definitely been here before. And if that wasn't scary enough, what was really, really scary was the fact that if he was where he knew he was, how on earth did he get here? It was then that his face went very pale and for a moment he thought his legs were going to buckle under him. I mean how do you explain being in Mr Vass's scrap yard one minute and the next you're eight thousand miles away, standing in the middle of Montana?

'Is everything all right constable?' asked Lizzie in a slightly worried voice. 'Only you've gone very pale again.'

'No, no I'm fine,' PC Goodrich replied, struggling to recover his composure.

Chapter Ten

US Seventh Cavalry

AND THEN HE heard it. The unmistakable drumming of horses' hooves and judging by the sound they were making, there were quite a lot of them too. Turning towards where the sound was coming from, PC Goodrich strained his eyes, hoping to catch sight of them. But all that met his gaze was an endless panorama of waving grass, stretching away to the distant horizon. But then suddenly something caught his eye, a flash of colour against the blue of the sky. His first thought was that it was a flag and although he hated to admit it, his second thought told him he was right. Not only that, but as the image became clearer, he found that he even recognised whose flag it was and this sent shivers down his back, for it not only confirmed exactly where they were but even what day it was.

'What's that noise?' asked Lizzie her ears picking up the sound.

'Horses.' PC Goodrich replied. 'And coming this way too.'

'I can't see anything.' said Sam staring in the general direction that PC Goodrich was looking in.

'There.' said PC Goodrich pointing with his arm.

'Oh I do see something' said Lizzie excitedly, 'but it's not a horse it's a … it's a flag I think.'

'Well you're almost correct young lady, but in fact it's called a guidon or more correctly a swallow-tailed guidon because it's shaped like a swallow's tail feathers.'

'What's it doing here?' enquired Sam butting in.

Turning to face the two children, PC Goodrich pondered for a moment on how best to answer the question, then deciding that it was probably best to be honest with them he replied calmly.

'If I'm right and on this occasion I most certainly am, that 'flag' as you call it belongs to the US Seventh Cavalry.'

The two children stared at him open-mouthed, neither able to speak a word.

'Which means,' said PC Goodrich, amazed that he could bring himself to admit it, 'that we really have travelled back in time as you said and we've arrived at the Little Bighorn in Montana and those horses over there are being ridden by the men of the seventh cavalry under the command of General George Armstrong Custer.' Pausing for a moment he went on, 'and if as I suspect the date today is the 25th of June 1876, then sadly they are all going to die.'

Horrified by this revelation, the two children stared at the column of riders as they drew closer, the blue of their uniforms visible now above the tall grass and the guidon with its red and white stripes with two circles of tiny gold stars set in a blue square, fluttering above them in the warm breeze.

Angry at himself for his last remark, PC Goodrich tucked the strap of his helmet under his chin.

'Right, time we made ourselves scarce I think. Follow me.'

And with that he set off at a brisk pace, brushing the tall grass aside like an ocean liner ploughing through a stormy sea. Without a word of dissent, their faces etched with concern, Sam and Lizzie hurried after him.

They hadn't gone too far though when Sam suddenly stopped dead in his tracks.

'Hold on,' he said, 'why are we running away?'

Lizzie, who had carried on walking, stopped and looked back at him, puffing out her cheeks in annoyance.

'Well it's not as if they can see us is it,' said Sam ignoring her disapproving look, 'we're invisible remember?'

'Gosh you're right,' said Lizzie suddenly recalling their encounter with the Saxon warriors at Sutton Hoo, 'I'd clean forgotten.'

Distracted by the sound of the children's voices, PC Goodrich halted and did a smart about turn, then beckoning with his hand, he said in an urgent voice.

'Come on! Come on! No time for chitter-chatter.'

With a smile of relief on her face Lizzie replied.

'It's all right constable, we've just remembered that they won't be able to see us, you see...'

'Nonsense!' said PC Goodrich interrupting her, 'of course they'll see us, they're not blind you know and if we don't....'

This time it was Sam's turn to interrupt.

'They didn't see us last time, so why should it be any different this time?'

Taken aback by Sam's words, PC Goodrich paused for a moment. It didn't make sense to him and yet both of the children seemed pretty sure of their facts.

'Perhaps you had better explain,' he said at last.

'Well,' said Sam, 'there was this rabbit and...,' pausing he looked across at Lizzie. 'You tell him Lizzie, you can explain it better than me.'

Lizzie smiled and turned to face PC Goodrich who stood looking at her expectantly.

'What Sam is trying to say is, that when we were at Sutton Hoo even a rabbit who hopped right up close couldn't see us, nor could any of the Saxon warriors. I think they could sense something was there but they definitely couldn't see us. Don't ask me why but it's true, honestly.'

PC Goodrich stared at Lizzie for a moment, then softening his expression he said.

'Very well, I believe you but....' he took a quick look at the approaching horsemen. 'But on this occasion I don't think we should assume anything, at least not until we're sure and so purely as a precaution I think we should err on the side of caution and keep out of sight.' And with that said he turned and strode away.

Seeing that the constable's mind was made up, Lizzie and Sam hurried after him.

Though they hated to admit it, he was probably right and besides who knows? Things might be different this time.

After catching up with PC Goodrich, the children were surprised when after only walking a short distance, the constable suddenly stopped in his tracks and taking a clean white handkerchief from one of his pockets he pushed back his helmet and began mopping his brow.

'Are you all right?' Lizzie asked, 'do you want to sit down again? Only your face does look a bit red.'

'No that won't be necessary, it's just the heat, takes a bit of getting used to that's all.'

'Maybe you should undo your top button after all,' said Sam trying to be helpful, 'we won't tell will we Lizzie?'

Lizzie looked at PC Goodrich and smiled.

'Sam's right, it might help.'

'Oh all right, I don't suppose it will do any harm.' And with that PC Goodrich pushed his handkerchief back into his pocket and undid the top button of his uniform.

'Hey look,' said Sam suddenly pointing back to where they had come from 'they're riding away. I told you they wouldn't see us didn't I?'

True enough when Lizzie and PC Goodrich turned to look they saw that the column of mounted soldiers were indeed riding past them and not a single head turned in their direction.

'If my memory serves me right, they're heading for Medicine Tail Coulee so that they can cross the river and attack the Indian village on the other side,' said PC Goodrich matter-of-factly.

Sam and Lizzie both stared at him with frowns on their faces.

'How do you know that?' asked Lizzie.' I mean where they are going and everything.'

'Ah well you see I've always been very keen on American history.'

'So we really are in America then?' exclaimed Sam, his face breaking into a broad smile. 'Wow, America, how amazing is that!'

'Be quiet Sam!' shouted Lizzie, sounding quite angry. Then turning back towards PC Goodrich she said in her most serious voice, 'That's all very well but I think there's something you're not telling us.'

Feeling guilty at being found out, PC Goodrich replied a little sheepishly,

'Yes I'm afraid you're right.'

Lizzie and Sam stared at him accusingly.

'Look,' said PC Goodrich, 'it's a bit of a long story so why don't we sit down here for a moment and I'll explain everything to you.'

Without uttering a word Sam and Lizzie plonked themselves down in the tall grass and with their chins resting in the palms of their hands they waited for PC Goodrich to begin.

'Well,' said PC Goodrich taking a deep breath, 'Before I came to Tingwick, quite a few years before in fact, I served as a mounted policeman with the Metropolitan Police Force in London.'

'Gee Whiz,' said Sam sounding quite amazed, 'you were a mounted policeman?'

'Yes,' said PC Goodrich, trying hard not to sound too indignant, 'hard though it may be for you to imagine, but yes I was a mounted policeman.'

Before Sam could utter another word, Lizzie frowned at him and put a finger across her lips.

Suitably put in his place, Sam gave a shrug of the shoulders and swallowed whatever it was that he was about to say.

'As I was saying,' said PC Goodrich, 'during my time with the Met I was fortunate enough to be sent on an exchange posting to the Canadian Mounted Police in Alberta Canada.'

'So you were a Mountie too?' This time it was Lizzie who interrupted.

'Yes I was, well for a month anyway,' said PC Goodrich grinning modestly.

'Did you get to wear a red jacket and a cowboy hat?' asked Sam excitedly.

'Yes.' said PC Goodrich. 'Now if you'll just let me finish.'

Pulling a face, Sam fell silent.

'Anyway,' PC Goodrich went on, 'while I was in Alberta I happened to mention to the family I was staying with that I was interested in the Wild West and in particular American Indians and so they kindly arranged a trip. Happily for me the American state which borders Alberta is Montana and so they took me to visit the Little Bighorn battlefield.

'And that's how you know where we are, you've been here before?' said Lizzie in amazement.

'Correct.' said PC Goodrich.

'Seems pretty spooky to me,' said Sam, unable to stay quiet for long, 'you having been here before I mean.'

PC Goodrich looked at Sam and grinned, 'Yes but not half as spooky as it is now,' he replied, 'on that occasion I came in a car and not a time machine.'

'So is it the same?' asked Lizzie, 'I mean, is it how it was when you were here last time?'

PC Goodrich thought for a moment and then after taking a quick look around him he said.

'Well of course lots of things were different then, for example there was a visitor centre and a monument but yes it's the same place all right, I'm certain.' Then shrugging his shoulders. 'It's just one of those places you never forget.'

'So what about those soldiers we just saw, how do you really know they are who you say they are?' said Sam feeling a little confused by the whole thing, 'I mean perhaps somebody's making a film or something and they're not really that General Custer at all.'

'Don't be stupid,' snapped Lizzie, 'there would be cameras and things.'

'No, no the boy's right,' said PC Goodrich, stopping her before she could go on.

'Perhaps I was wrong in jumping to conclusions. I mean just because I said I knew who they were, it doesn't necessarily mean that they are 'THE' Seventh Cavalry.' And then suddenly a thought struck him and jumping to his feet he said excitely. 'But there is a way to prove it one way or the other.'

The two children stared up at him, totally bemused.

'Well don't just sit there, come on follow me.'

And with that PC Goodrich pulled on his domed helmet, tucked the strap under his chin and set off as fast as his legs would carry him towards the brow of the hill which, the troop of cavalry had disappeared behind.

In a flash Lizzie and Sam were up on their feet and hurrying after him.

'I think he must have sunstroke or something,' said Sam as the pair broke into a run, 'he's probably never been here before and he's just imagining it all.'

'Oh I don't think so,' Lizzie replied hurrying to catch up with the constable, 'anyway it looks like we're soon going to find out for sure.'

With a cooling breeze at their backs and the midday sun hanging over them in a cloudless blue sky, the three time travellers reached the brow of the hill and stopped.

Without saying a word, Sam and Lizzie each reached out and took hold of one of PC Goodrich's hands and instinctively the policeman gave each of them a reassuring squeeze. Below them at the foot of the hill was the Little Bighorn River, called by the Indians the Greasy Grass but what held their attention was not the slowly flowing river but what was on the far bank.

Chapter Eleven

The Little Bighorn River

TEPEES. HUNDREDS AND hundreds of them, stretching along the far bank of the river for over half a mile, each one decorated with its own distinctive markings, some with images of buffalo and horses while other less decorative ones were painted with small clusters of falling stars or a single buffalo hide shield painted on one panel. A kaleidoscope of shapes and colours which took their breath away. And as if that were not enough, just as impressive was the Indians' pony herd. Too many to count, they covered the hillside behind the village like a multi-coloured carpet; Duns, Appaloosa, Buckskins and Piebalds, truly a horse lover's dream come true.

Staring speechless at the scene before them, it was PC Goodrich's voice which broke the silence and although he felt he should have said more, all that escaped his lips was a single word.

'Incredible!'

Sam was next to speak and although he too could only manage one word, to his credit he did make it sound like three.

'A-maz-ing!'

Lizzie remained silent, her gaze fixed on the far bank, although clearly astonished by what she was witnessing, whatever her thoughts were it seemed for now she was keeping them to herself.

In the village, crowds of young children ran about among the tepees while their mothers and grandmothers busied themselves around the cooking fires. The few warriors that could be seen were gathered in small groups, the smoke from their pipes drifting upwards in the still air.

Turning away at last, Lizzie looked up at PC Goodrich and said in a quiet voice,

'It seems you were right after all.'

'Well yes I suppose I was,' replied PC Goodrich, not exactly feeling over the moon with the admission. 'This is definitely the Little Bighorn and that is the largest gathering of Sioux and Cheyenne Indians anyone is ever going to see.'

No sooner had he spoken, when suddenly struck by the realization of what he had just said, PC Goodrich let out a groan and with his legs turning to jelly, he flopped down onto the ground pulling the two startled children with him.

Letting go of PC Goodrich's hand, like a well-rehearsed double act, Sam immediately removed the constable's helmet while Lizzie undid the top button of his uniform.

'He's gone all pale again,' said Sam peering into PC Goodrich's face.

'He'll be all right in a minute,' said Lizzie reassuringly, 'it's all a bit of a shock to him I suppose.'

'It's a bit of a shock to me too,' said Sam 'but....'

'Yes but you have to remember he hasn't got over the time travel bit yet and now all this, well it must be a bit unsettling for someone who's old.'

'Old!' PC Goodrich blurted out, 'I'll have you know I've a good few years yet before I hang up my truncheon,' and then he fell silent. This was all really getting a bit much for him he concluded.

Seeing the dejected expression on his face, Lizzie put a hand on PC Goodrich's shoulder and said as reassuringly as she could.

'I didn't really mean you were old,' said Lizzie, frantically racking her brain for a suitably sympathetic reply. 'I just meant that you were, well not as young as us.'

With his indignation soothed a little by Lizzie's words, PC Goodrich climbed unsteadily to his feet.

'Well that's all right then, don't want you to think that because I'm a few,…err quite a few years your senior that I'm letting the side down,' adding a little reluctantly, 'of course it has all been a bit of a shock,' then tugging at his uniform collar, 'and there's the heat of course and this uniform is, well shall we say, it's not ideally suited for hot climates.'

With Sam having trouble suppressing the laugh which threatened to burst from his mouth and before Lizzie could acknowledge just how hot it was, a popping sound, like dozens of bangers exploding on firework night broke the silence.

In an instant the three of them turned their gaze onto the village and open-mouthed they watched in amazement as its quiet composure was shattered by people suddenly running about in all directions, their cries of alarm carrying across the river.

'Reno', said PC Goodrich.

'Reno?' said Lizzie. But before she could ask her question, PC Goodrich went on;

'Captain Marcus Reno, was Custer's second in command and I think the gunfire...'

'Look!' shouted Sam, cutting PC Goodrich off in mid-sentence, 'the Indians are getting on their horses.'

Sure enough, when Lizzie and the constable looked back at the village, dozens of warriors clutching rifles and lances were mounting their ponies, while behind the village more warriors and young boys were rounding up ponies and herding them into the village.

'Is there going to be a battle?' cried Sam excitedly.

'Yes,' replied PC Goodrich 'but this is not it. This is just the start.'

Sam looked at him with a puzzled expression on his face.

'Look,' said PC Goodrich, feeling a little excited himself now, 'we're pretty safe up here, so why don't we go and see for ourselves and then I can explain.'

And with that, PC Goodrich turned on his heels and with what passed for running, keeping the Little Bighorn River on his right, he hurried away along the top of the hill.

Sam and Lizzie stared at each other for a moment and then with a shrug of the shoulder they chased after him.

Chapter Twelve

Reno Attacks

N O SOONER HAD Lizzie and Sam caught up with PC Goodrich when, crossing over to a rocky outcrop, he dropped down onto one knee and with a wave of his hand he signalled for them to join him.

'This should do,' he said a little out of breath, 'we can get a good view of things from here.'

Making their way to the pile of boulders, Sam and Lizzie squatted down beside PC Goodrich and peered down at the scene below them.

A wide meadow ran alongside the river, its steep bank covered in dense clumps of trees and off to the right they could just see the tepees at the far end of the village.

Then hardly daring to believe their eyes, the two children watched spellbound as an extended line of mounted troopers suddenly galloped into view.

'Those,' said PC Goodrich are A.G.and M. companies under the command of Major Reno and their orders are to attack the Indian village from the south.'

No sooner had he finished speaking when for no apparent reason, the charging horsemen suddenly reigned in their mounts and with each fourth trooper holding their horses, the other three troopers, each armed with a rifle, formed a long skirmish line.

'What are they doing?' shouted Sam, 'why are they getting off their horses?'

'I think that's why,' cried Lizzie pointing towards the village, 'look the Indians are coming to attack them.'

Sure enough, just as Lizzie had said, suddenly hundreds of warriors, mounted on their ponies, rode out from among the tepees and yelling their war-cries they galloped at speed towards the line of soldiers.

'Those are Hunkpapa,' said PC Goodrich excitedly, 'and a pound to a penny that's a chief called Rain-in-the-Face leading them.'

'Hunkpapa! I thought you said they were called Sioux?' said Sam.

'They are Sioux' PC Goodrich replied, quite put out that Sam didn't know the names of the Sioux tribes. 'Don't you children play cowboys and Indians anymore?'

But Sam wasn't listening, being totally engrossed in what was happening on the open grassland across the river.

The sound of gunfire was much louder now, with most of it coming from the blue coated soldiers, as again and again bands of warriors charged headlong towards them firing with their bows and arrows as well as rifles. Several Indians were hit and fell onto the ground, their riderless ponies racing away to safety.

'The soldiers are winning.' shouted Sam excitedly.

But just as he spoke, an Indian, mounted on an Appaloosa pony, began shouting out to the warriors around him and then kicking his pony into a run, he dashed away towards the far end of the skirmish line. Whooping and yelling, most of the attacking Indians rode after him, while the remainder turned and rode towards the trees alongside the riverbank.

'They're running away.' said Lizzie sounding quite dejected.

'Far from it young lady. No they've worked out that it's too dangerous to charge at the soldiers like that so their war chief is leading them around the skirmish line so they can get behind the soldiers and attack them from the rear.'

Almost as if he had overheard what PC Goodrich had said, alarmed by the Indians' proposed tactic, kicking his horse into a gallop, Major Reno rode along the skirmish line and calling out in a loud voice he ordered his troopers to mount up and retreat back towards where they had crossed the river.

Obeying their commander's order and with the bugler sounding the retreat, the troopers climbed back into their saddles and raced away from the village, each of them eager to get across the river and make a stand on the high ground beyond.

But as they galloped desperately towards the crossing point scores of warriors, mounted on their swift war-ponies, swooped down on them and at least a dozen troopers were hit and fell from their horses.

'Right children time for us to leave,' said PC Goodrich a little concerned by the unfolding events.

Pulling a face Sam grumbled. 'But it's just getting exciting.'

'No buts young lad', said PC Goodrich in a firm voice, pointing with his arm towards the river bank below them, 'I think those warriors down there are getting a little too close for comfort.'

Looking down to where PC Goodrich was pointing, Sam and Lizzie saw a tall young Indian, his handsome face daubed with war-paint, followed by a large group of mounted warriors, each of them armed with a rifle, splashing across the shallow river.

Smiling brightly Lizzie turned to the constable and said in her most reassuring voice,

'Oh you don't have to worry about them, like Sam and I said, they won't be able to see us because we're invisible.'

'Yes, yes so you keep telling me but while that's all very well if you're right,' said PC

Goodrich not at all convinced about this whole invisible thing, 'if you're wrong, well in case you hadn't noticed, but I'm wearing a blue uniform!'

The two children looked at one another and deciding that nothing they said or did was going to change PC Goodrich's mind, they turned their backs on the river and began walking away towards the Indian village.

'What do we do now then?' said Sam trying not to sound too disgruntled.

Before anyone could answer his question, the sound of heavy gunfire came from somewhere up ahead of them, followed by the clarion call of a bugle. Instinctively, both Sam and Lizzie turned their heads and looked up enquiringly at PC Goodrich.

Smiling at the questioning look on each of their faces, PC Goodrich said, 'so I'm supposed to know everything am I?'

'Well you did say you knew quite a lot about American history,' Lizzie reminded him.

'Yes,' said Sam enthusiastically, 'and you've been spot on so far, I mean knowing about Major Reno and those Hunkpapa.'

Taking a moment to replace his helmet, PC Goodrich gathered his thoughts.

Well,' he said after a moment's deliberation, 'I'm quite surprised you haven't worked it out for yourselves.'

'What do you mean?' said Lizzie, puzzled by his remark.

'Well surely you must have a pretty good idea where we are?'

'Yes,' said Sam, 'we're in Montana, or so you say and there's some sort of battle going on between the soldiers and the Indians.'

'So you've really no idea?' said PC Goodrich totally amazed by Sam's reply. And then staring into Sam's face he went on, 'I thought being a boy you were sure to have heard of the battle of the Little Bighorn.'

'No,' said Sam with a shrug of his shoulders, 'I've never heard of any Little Bighorn, not until now anyway.'

'Well blow me down!' PC Goodrich exclaimed, completely amazed.

Watching them, her forehead creased in a frown, Lizzie suddenly cried out in an excited voice, 'The guidon! You said it belonged to

General Custer! This is Custer's Last Stand isn't it?'

'Well done young lady. Well done, at least somebody has been paying attention,' said PC Goodrich, giving Sam a disappointed look.

'Well how was I to know that they were the same thing?' moaned Sam not looking at all happy. 'Of course I've heard of Custer's Last Stand, my Mum and Dad went to see the film when it was on at the pictures but it wasn't called the battle of the Little Bighorn.'

'Yes I suppose it has all got a bit confusing,' said PC Goodrich giving Sam a smile,

Hollywood has a lot to answer for. Anyway not to worry, at least we all know where we are now, that's the main thing.'

'So does all that noise mean that Custer is being attacked?' Lizzie asked, a look of concern crossing her face as the sound of gunfire grew louder and the sound of the bugle rang out again.

'Yes I'm afraid so,' said PC Goodrich. Then pointing with his arm he went on. 'Just behind that low hill over there he and his men are making their last stand.'

'Can we go and see?' shouted Sam excitedly.

'No, I don't think that's a very good idea,' PC Goodrich replied.

'Why, what harm can it do?' said Sam, clearly put out by the constable's reply. 'I mean it's not as if they will even see us.'

PC Goodrich looked straight-faced at Sam, 'That's as maybe but it's not what they can or can't see that bothers me, it's what you two will see that concerns me. Men are being killed over there and I don't imagine for one minute that it's a very pretty sight.'

'We've seen a dead man before haven't we Lizzie?' said Sam puffing out his chest.

Lizzie slowly nodded her head.

'When my Granddad died,' Sam went on, 'his coffin was put on our dining room table and we all went to see him and we weren't scared at all. My sister Debbie even kissed him, right on his lips.'

'Yes,' said Lizzie, giving him a disapproving look, 'and you still managed to eat most of the cheese and watercress sandwiches too.'

PC Goodrich smiled and looked at the two children. It was clear to him that they weren't going to be put off, so reluctantly with a shrug of his shoulders he gave in.

'Very well then, perhaps if we don't get too close,' said PC Goodrich, 'and you both promise not to behave like babies, it should be all right I suppose.'

Immediately Sam and Lizzie's faces lit up.

'But!' said PC Goodrich in a stern voice, 'you do exactly as I say, do you hear me?'

'Yes constable,' Sam and Lizzie replied in unison, both grinning from ear to ear.

Still not convinced that he was doing the right thing but secretly wanting to go and take a look for himself as much as the children did, with Sam and Lizzie close by his side, PC Goodrich made his way towards the low hill and the sound of battle.

Chapter Thirteen

Custer's Last Stand

THE WALK TOOK longer than expected with PC Goodrich saying at one point that he wished he had managed to bring his trusty bike with him. But eventually they drew nearer to the sound of battle and as they did so they suddenly saw large numbers of warriors mounted on their war-ponies, galloping up the slope of the hill from all directions, waving their rifles and lances in the air and shrieking their war-cries.

Spotting a narrow ravine overgrown with bushes, PC Goodrich grabbed hold of Sam and Lizzie by the hand and hurried towards it. Hidden by the foliage, the three time travellers moved forward cautiously, the crash of gunfire and the sound of war-cries was almost deafening. At last they reached the top of the ravine and dropping to the ground they crawled forward on their hands and knees until they reached a point where they could see the battlefield.

Nobody spoke as wide-eyed they took in the scene before them. Scattered across the hillside were groups of blue-coated soldiers, some still mounted on their horses', with others standing or kneeling behind their fallen horses and using them as barricades. Everywhere, wave after wave of Sioux and Cheyenne warriors, their faces and bodies daubed in war paint circled around them, charging forward on their ponies and firing at point blank range at the terrified soldiers. At first nobody spoke, each of them staring wide-eyed in amazement as the battle raged around them. Then Sam called out, his voice full of excitement.

'Did you see that?' he shouted, pointing towards two Indians on painted ponies as they galloped across the hillside in front of them, 'those two Indians charged right up to the soldiers and just touched them with their lances and rode off.'

'It's called counting coup,' said PC Goodrich, a fount of knowledge where these things were concerned, 'apparently it's a sign of bravery among the Plains Indians.'

'Seems a pretty daft thing to do to me,' said Sam, 'with all those soldiers shooting at them.'

'Well that's as maybe my boy but it still takes a lot of courage to do it all the same.'

'Where's General Custer?' Lizzie suddenly called out.

Absorbed by the battle PC Goodrich leaned towards her and pointed up towards the crown of the hill.

'Do you see the guidon, there at the very top of the hill?'

Lizzie strained her eyes. 'Yes, I can see it.'

'Well,' said PC Goodrich, 'can you see the man standing to the right of it?'

'Who? the one in the light coloured jacket?'

'Yes.' Well that's General Custer, he nearly always wore a buckskin jacket, I suppose it made it easy for his men to spot him in a battle.'

'Look!' shouted Sam, 'more Indians are coming.'

Sure enough, just as Sam spoke, at least a hundred mounted Indians, their eagle-feather headdresses streaming out behind them, appeared over the crest of the next hill and whooping and yelling, the hooves of their war-ponies drumming on the dry ground, they galloped towards the groups of encircled soldiers.

'I can't be sure,' shouted PC Goodrich, 'but that could be Crazy Horse and his Ogalalas'.

No sooner had he spoken when suddenly, led by two mounted officers, about thirty soldiers, most of them on foot, broke away from the main body and made a dash towards a narrow gully, which led down to the Bighorn River. In an instant Crazy Horse spotted them and signalling to his warriors, he wheeled his pony around and raced towards them. When all but two of the soldiers had reached the gully, the officer, mounted on a buckskin horse, seeing Crazy Horse and his warriors riding towards them, shouted to his men to stand their ground. A few of the braver soldiers obeyed his command and turning to face the charging Indians, they fired a volley into them before turning and running down the gully with the rest of the terrified troopers.

Several Indians were hit by the soldiers' bullets and fell from their ponies but the rest came on and in seconds they had overrun the hated blue-coats who had come to attack their village.

'I think some of the soldiers are getting away,' shouted Sam excitedly.

'Oh I do hope so,' cried Lizzie.

But as they watched, the two children saw their hopes dashed, as mounted on their nimble ponies, the Sioux warriors rode them down, firing at the fleeing troopers with their rifles and spearing them with their lances.

At first, PC Goodrich thought Lizzie might burst into tears but as he was soon to discover, she was made of tougher stuff than he thought.

Finally, deciding that they had seen enough, looking back down the ravine where they were hiding and seeing that it was all clear, PC Goodrich called out to the two children.

'Right come along you two, I think it's time we left.'

No sooner had he spoken when Lizzie, who was still watching the fighting, caught sight of the officer mounted on the buckskin horse encircled by a crowd of Indians.

Slashing left and right with his sabre, he spurred his horse forward. Sadly before he could fight his way through the mounted Indians swirling around him, a warrior wearing a long flowing headdress raised his rifle and fired at him from point blank range. Fatally wounded by the bullet in his chest, the officer fell from his saddle. Whooping with triumph, the warrior kicked his pony forward and reaching out he grabbed the cavalry horse's reigns. Instantly Lizzie let out a loud scream and before either Sam or PC Goodrich could stop her, she jumped up and ran as fast as she could towards the gully. Watching in horror, PC Goodrich clambered to his feet and with Sam a step behind him, he chased after her.

Gripping the buckskin's reigns tightly in his hand, pleased with his prize, the Sioux warrior kicked his heels into his pony's flanks and galloped away. With the pony and its rider bearing down on her, fearlessly Lizzie stood her ground and as they drew nearer she began waving her arms in the air and screaming out at the top of her voice. At first nothing happened, then when the pony was almost on top of her, whinnying with fear, it suddenly veered away. Caught out by the pony's sudden change of direction, its rider was flung from its back and with the bay's reigns snatched from his hands, he crashed onto the ground and lay still. Panting from exertion, PC Goodrich arrived at Lizze's side.

'What the devil are you playing at?' he shouted, 'you could....' And then his jaw dropped and he stood staring in amazement at the buckskin horse standing in front of him, its huge liquid brown eyes looking right at him.

'He can't see us of course,' said Sam matter-of-factly, 'but he knows something's not quite right.'

'He's not as frightened as that pony was,' said Lizzie.

'Lucky for you that pony was scared, or it would have trampled all over you.'

Sam remarked, a little miffed that he hadn't been the one to go to the horse's rescue.

Then before Lizzie could reply, as if Sam's voice had broken the spell, the buckskin swung its neck around and trotted away.

'Right!' said PC Goodrich, his composure restored, 'now we really have to.' Then he fell silent and a puzzled expression began spreading across his face. Sam and Lizzie noticed it too, suddenly everything around them was becoming blurred and out of focus. Instantly they knew what was happening and quick as a flash, just as everything began to go dark, they each took hold of one of PC Goodrich's hands and Sam shouted out at the top of his voice.

'Hold on! Hold on tight.'

Chapter Fourteen

Home Again

THIS TIME THERE was no wondering where they were, because the rest room was just as they had left it (whenever that was). Nothing had changed, nothing was out of place, even the Watling Rol-A-Top was still standing in the corner, like a faithful dog waiting patiently for its master's return.

'Well here we are, home again safe and sound,' said Sam more relieved than he cared to admit.

Lizzie didn't say anything, she was too busy looking at PC Goodrich, who had flopped down on the battered sofa, his normally pale cheeks quite flushed.

'Well who would have believed it?' PC Goodrich said, his face blossoming into a smile.

'Nobody,' Sam replied, 'whoever we told they would think we were making it all up, just like you did when we told you.'

'Yes,' said PC Goodrich, feeling a little embarrassed, 'but you have to admit it did all sound pretty farfetched.'

'Are you glad you pulled the handle constable?' Lizzie asked, changing the subject.

'But of course,' said PC Goodrich, 'wouldn't have missed it for the world.'

Sam and Lizzie looked at each other and smiled.

'So we're not going to get into trouble then?' asked Sam.

PC Goodrich looked up at the children and tried to look serious but the smile on his face wouldn't budge.

'No not on this occasion, after all you were accompanied by an adult, so if anybody is to blame I suppose it's me.'

'We won't tell anybody will we Sam?' said Lizzie very relieved to hear that they were in the clear.

Sam shook his head vigorously.

But PC Goodrich's thoughts were already elsewhere.

'The Battle of the Little Bighorn and we were there to see it. Remarkable, quite remarkable,' he said, a faraway look in his eyes. Then gazing up at Lizzie he added, 'and where, believe it or not young lady, you may very well have made history, or at the very least changed it.'

'What ever do you mean?' asked Lizzie sounding a little nervous.

PC Goodrich gave a little chuckle, 'Don't sound so worried you didn't do anything wrong, quite the opposite in fact.'

Lizzie and Sam stared at each other and then looked back at PC Goodrich.

'Come and sit down the pair of you,' said the constable patting the sofa, 'and I'll tell you a quite remarkable story.'

With the two children sitting on each side of him on the battered sofa, glancing across at Lizzie PC Goodrich began.

'Do you remember when you quite foolishly ran out and frightened that Indian's pony?'

'The one who had just killed the officer and taken his horse?' said Sam butting in.

'Yes that's the one, said PC Goodrich, 'Well as it happens that horse, the one the Indian was making off with belonged to a Captain Myles Keogh.'

'How come you know that?' asked Sam, his curiosity as always getting the better of him.

'If you'll just let me finish,' said PC Goodrich, 'you'll find out. Now where was I?…, Oh yes Captain Keogh. Well as it happens I recognised him from some regimental photographs I'd seen in a book. Did either of you happen to notice that the officer we saw had a very distinctive goatee beard and moustache?'

Sam and Lizzie both shook their heads.

'Well he did and so too did Captain Keogh and as I'm pretty sure there were no other officers in Custer's Command with similar facial hair, I think it's fair to say that it was definitely Captain Keogh we saw riding the horse that you saved.'

'Satisfied!' hissed Lizzie, glaring at Sam.

'Anyway,' PC Goodrich went on, 'two days after the battle, Captain Keogh's horse, who was called Comanche by the way, was found and although he was quite badly wounded, with everyone else, soldiers and horses, all killed, thanks to you young lady, he was the only survivor of Custer's Last Stand.'

'Wow,' said Sam, 'that's really something.'

'So what happened to him after that?' said Lizzie, totally intrigued by the story.

'Well as you might expect, he became quite famous, in fact for a long time afterwards he was the most famous horse in America. The soldiers loved him of course and when he had recovered from his wounds, he was retired with honour and the order was given that he was never to be ridden again.'

'Good for him,' Sam chipped in, 'he deserved it didn't he Lizzie?'

Lizzie looked at him and tried her best to smile. While she was thrilled that Comanche's story had a happy ending, strangely a part of her was also a little sad.

'Hey why the long face?' said Sam a little puzzled by Lizzie's glum expression. 'If it hadn't been for you he would probably have been killed.'

'The lad's right,' PC Goodrich confirmed, 'once that Indian warrior found out that the soldier's horse was badly wounded, he might very well have shot him.'

'Yes I know,' said Lizzie, 'it's just that.' And then she fell silent.

'Just what?' said Sam.

'Well' Lizzie replied, feeling a little embarrassed, 'I know it sounds stupid but I just wish that I could have seen him once more that's all.'

'What if I told you you could?' said PC Goodrich matter of factly.

'What!' shouted Sam, 'you mean he's still alive?'

'Don't be stupid, horses can't live that long.' snapped Lizzie. Then turning to PC Goodrich, with a tiny hint of doubt in her voice she said, 'I mean they just can't can they?'

'No sadly they can't young lady.' PC Goodrich replied, doing his best to keep a straight face. 'I mean if Comanche were still alive today that would make him.' He paused for a moment. 'Hummm let's see now, if we say he was fourteen at the Battle of the Little Bighorn and that was fought in 1876 and it's now 1965...' A minute or so of theatrical mental arithmetic, accompanied by some finger counting followed before he finally concluded by saying. 'If my maths are correct, by my reckoning that would make him one hundred and three.'

Clearly not at all amused by PC Goodrich's childish behaviour, Sam and Lizzie folded their arms across their chests and glared at him disapprovingly.

Seeing his attempt at humour fall on stony ground, PC Goodrich cleared his throat and went on. 'What I meant was, if you really did want to see him again, you can, because he is in a glass display case in the Natural History Museum at the University of Kansas.'

Lizzie went so pale that Sam thought for a moment that she was going to pass out but then a faint smile crept back onto her face.

'He must have been very special for them to go to all that trouble.'

'He most certainly was young lady, there will never be another one like him that's for sure.' said PC Goodrich.' Then suddenly conscious of the time, he reached into his top pocket and removing a silver pocket watch he opened the case.

'Goodness is that the time?' he exclaimed, quite surprised that it was so late, 'time I was back at the station.'

His first and second attempt to get up from the sofa failed, so it was left to Sam and Lizzie to take hold of an arm each and haul PC Goodrich up onto his feet.

'Right you two,' he said in his official policeman's voice, 'this is to remain our secret. Understood?'

Hardly daring to believe what he had just said, Sam and Lizzie both blurted out 'yes!' at the same time.

'And we'll meet here on the third Saturday of each month at twelve o'clock sharp, agreed?'

Grinning from ear to ear the two children stared at PC Goodrich and nodded their heads vigorously.

'Oh and it might be a good idea to bring a few sandwiches next time,' said the constable, brushing the dust off the sleeve of his uniform before adding, 'I don't know about you two but all this travelling through time tends to make me very hungry.'

Once the three of them were outside the engine shed, PC Goodrich slipped the key to the rest room into his uniform pocket and without another word, he climbed onto his bicycle and cycled away. Watching him go Sam couldn't help but smile.

'And what are you looking so pleased about?' asked Lizzie, digging him in the ribs with her elbow.

'Oh I was just thinking,' Sam replied through gritted teeth.

'Thinking what?' said Lizzie.

'That old PC Goodrich is not such a bad sort after all.'

No sooner had Sam spoken, when just before he disappeared out of sight through the scrap yard gates, PC Goodrich called out in a loud voice.

'Mind you don't go getting into any mischief.'

Chapter Fifteen

All Good Things

SAM, LIZZIE AND PC Goodrich never did go back to the rest room in the engine shed.

On the following Sunday PC Goodrich's landlady Mrs Mardon took him his early morning cup of tea, as she always did when he was off duty and found that he had passed away in his sleep. After the funeral she told everyone that he had died peacefully with a smile on his face and although most people didn't give it a second thought, Sam and Lizzie liked to think that the reason he was smiling was because he was remembering their adventure together.

In accordance with his wishes, PC Goodrich was buried in his police constable's uniform along with his silver pocket watch and of course the key to the rest room. Sam had said that it didn't matter about the key and that they could quite easily force the door open any time they wanted to. But as the days became weeks and the weeks turned into months, they never did go back to the scrap yard. It didn't seem right somehow, not without PC Goodrich.

A year later Mr Vass also passed away. Old Charlie had found him slumped in his battered old office chair with a faded photograph of his son Vic clutched in his hand.

Soon after that the scrap yard was sold to a property developer and it wasn't long before the bulldozers moved in and within a week all that remained of the scrap yard was a giant mound of rubble and piles of mangled metal. Several of the men working in the demolition crew had served in the army and so they were amazed and delighted to find an old Sherman tank and half a dozen Bren Gun Carriers hidden away in one of the old buildings. Strangely though, no mention was ever made of anybody finding a brightly coloured Watling Rol-A-Top.

In her last year at school, Lizzie joined a pen-pal club and began corresponding to an American girl named Billie Lou who it turned out, just happened to live in Kansas.

Two years and several hundred letters later, thanks to a small inheritance from her Uncle Charlie, Lizzie boarded a plane at Heathrow and flew on a trip of a lifetime to meet her American pen-pal. Thankfully the pair got on famously and when Lizzie said she wanted to visit the University of Kansas, although a little surprised that she wanted to go on her own, Billy Lou's parents nevertheless made all the necessary arrangements. So on the following Saturday, the third of the month, just as she had always planned it, Lizzie climbed the stairs of the Natural History Museum to the fifth floor and at precisely twelve o'clock she came face to face with Comanche for the second time.

Enclosed in a huge glass display case, just as PC Goodrich had said, he looked exactly as she remembered him; standing tall, ears pricked, his saddle, stirrups and reigns freshly polished and wearing his dark blue cavalry blanket embroidered with the number seven. Looking once more into his big amber eyes, just for a moment she was transported back to the Little Bighorn and the moment when she had saved his life. With her emotions welling up inside her Lizzie quickly opened her bag and took out her camera. Photo taken, Lizzie put her camera away and stood admiring the display. She would have two prints taken, one for herself and one for Sam of course. It was his birthday in two weeks time and she never knew what to get him, boy was he in for a big surprise this birthday she thought.

Eventually, after staring at the beautiful buckskin horse for what seemed like ages, with her sadness hidden behind a bright smile, Lizzie placed her hand on the glass just inches from Comanche's nose and whispered goodbye.

Chapter Sixteen

Mystery Solved

I T WAS JUST beginning to get dark when Hamish McGregor spotted the familiar signpost and, turning off the main A84 he set off along the single track road to the small village of Stronvar.

After climbing up the steep incline, before he had gone half a mile the road was suddenly hemmed in on both sides by a dense avenue of fir trees, plunging it into darkness. Muttering something unmentionable under his breath, Hamish changed down into third gear. Then running his left hand along the dashboard he switched on the van's lights. Instantly, the road up ahead was bathed in a pale yellow light. Well half of it was. The bulb in the left headlight had blown a few months back and, despite

Hamish's good intentions, it was still waiting to be replaced.

Not that he needed lights to find his way. Over the years Hamish had driven along this same stretch of road more times than he cared to remember and, he knew every inch of it by heart. The old 1950's Transit van was no stranger to the road either. In fact Hamish often joked that if he ever fell asleep at the wheel, the old van could find its way home on its own.

Reaching the bend in the road where it turned to follow the course of the river, in ten minutes Hamish reached Stranvar. Many of the of stone cottages which lined the road were in darkness but here and there the soft glow of an oil lamp showed itself at a window. After leaving the village, Hamish turned off onto the Loch road. To be honest it was no more than a track really, more suited to tractors and 4 x 4's than an ageing van with a worn-out clutch and dodgy brakes. Cursing every bump and rut, Hamish finally reached the entrance to his croft.

The stout wooden gate which had once barred its entrance had long since disappeared and all that remained were the two wooden posts which had supported it. After driving a short distance, pushing his left foot down hard on the brake pedal while at the same time yanking hard on the handbrake, Hamish brought the van to a screeching halt. Home at last.

He had inherited the small croft on the banks of Loch Voit from his uncle Angus. The old man had been a bit of a recluse and, with no children of his own to leave it to, as his only living relative, it had passed to Hamish. Remote and isolated though it was, the small farm suited Hamish perfectly. Just like his uncle he too had never married. There had been a girl once. He had met her during his time in the army, when he and a pal had spent a few days of their leave in Blackpool. The two had written to each other when he returned to his regiment in Germany. But sadly for Hamish, horrified at the thought of her daughter marrying a soldier, her mother convinced her to end the romance. A week later Hamish received a 'Dear John' letter telling him that it was over between them.

His uncle kept a small flock of Blackface sheep on the farm. But after giving it a try for a few months, Hamish decided that being a shepherd wasn't for him and he sold them. Instead, to earn a living, he travelled around the local area doing odd jobs; Fixing roofs, building stone walls, that sort of thing. Making just enough money to pay the bills and, purchase the occasional bottle of malt whiskey.

Instead of pulling up outside the farmhouse, Hamish had parked outside an old stone barn built into the hillside. Switching off the ignition, he climbed out and walked around to the rear of the van. Removing the rusting padlock which held them shut, he pulled open the back doors and peered inside. Relieved to see that his cargo had survived the final leg of the journey without mishap, Hamish strode across to the door of the barn. Slipping a large brass key into the keyhole, he unlocked the solid wooden door. Propping it open with a large stone, Hamish then returned to the back of the van and, planting his a size eleven boot on the bumper, he hauled himself inside.

His 'acquisition' as he liked to call it was coved in a tarpaulin sheet, held firmly in place by a length of strong rope. With each end tied securely to two metal rings welded to the floor, it had barely moved an inch. Untying the rope, Hamish climbed out of the van and, gripping each of the two ends in his hands, he dragged the hidden object towards him. Freeing the rope, Hamish then wrapped both arms around the tarpaulin and, with a mighty heave, he lifted his 'acquisition' from the back of the Transit van and carried it into the gloomy interior of the shed.

To most men in their late sixties the prospect of single-handedly lifting up a Watling Rol-A-Top would have seemed unthinkable. But not to Hamish McGregor. Mind you at the age of twenty two he did win both the hammer throw and the Caber toss at the Highland games at Dunoon. So to anyone who remembered him achieving this impressive feat, the fact that he could man-handle such a heavy machine would have come as no surprise at all.

With the one arm bandit gripped in a bear-hug, Hamish carried it to the back of the shed and, set in down carefully in a vacant corner. After locking the door and with the key safely deposited in his jacket pocket, Hamish climbed back in the van. Releasing the handbrake, he then free-wheeled down the slope, eventually bringing the trusty van to halt outside the front door of the old farmhouse.

So how you might ask, did a Scottish crofter like Hamish McGregor come to be in possession of such a machine. Well to answer this, we have to go back to a particularly wet and windy day a month earlier. Looking to get out of the rain, Hamish had ventured into the public library in Callander and, picking up a copy of the Glasgow Herald, a small advertisement caught his eye;

Men experienced in demolition wanted. Good rates of pay. Please contact MacCormack & Son. Telephone Glasgow 712 713.

During his time in the army, Hamish had served in the REME (The Royal Electrical & Mechanical Engineers). So with years of experience in building bridges and driving bulldozers and cranes, working on the assumption that if you could put things up you could just as easily knock them down, Hamish called the number. Two weeks later and, after a short but successful interview, Hamish and his trusty van were on their way south of the border to the village of Tingwick.

Even as a lad Hamish had always been a bit of a magpie. Always happy to poke around and see what treasures he could find. So it came as no surprise that he was instinctively drawn to the engine shed. Most of the tools and bits of engines were to pitted and corroded to be of much use. But when he entered the small office and discovered what was lurking under the sheet of tarpaulin his face lit up. Delighted with his find and with the rest of the demolition crew away enjoying a well-earned pint or two in the local pub, unnoticed, Hamish loaded the one arm bandit onto the van and drove away. A month later, with Mr Vass's scrap yard reduced to a pile of rubble, a nice wad of cash in his wallet and his 'bonus' safely hidden in the back of his van, Hamish headed up the Great North Road to Scotland.

Of course he had every intention of finding a buyer for the fruit machine. But although he wouldn't admit it, over the years Hamish had become something of a hoarder and, like all hoarders' he was loathed to get rid of anything. Especially something as valuable as a Watling Rol-A-Top. So there it sat covered by its tarpaulin. And week after week, month after month, year after year, more and more of Hamish's finds piled up around it.

Nobody knew for sure how the old Transit van, with Hamish McGregor still sitting behind the wheel had ended up in the Loch. An angler out fishing found it early one morning, submerged in six feet of water. A set of muddy tracks showing where it had left the narrow road and careered down the steep hillside before plunging into the icy waters of the Loch. Some of the locals said old Hamish had probably had a few too many drams of whiskey. While others blamed the tragedy on the van's brakes, or rather the lack of them. The autopsy that followed proved both theories wrong. Its findings revealing that Hamish McGregor had simply suffered a fatal heart attack.

With no next of kin to inherit it, the croft stood empty and abandoned for the next five years. But thankfully, a rare visit to the post office by Mr McDuff a local solicitor was to save it from falling into ruin. Following a conversation with the postmaster on the subject of stamp collecting, a hobby which both men enjoyed, the postmaster suddenly recalled that Hamish once received a letter from Canada. It had been many years ago, but he distinctly remembered the letter and the post mark too. Toronto!

As trustee of Hamish's affairs Mr McDuff immediately placed an enquiry notice in the Toronto Star. A fortnight later a letter arrived from a firm of solicitors in Toronto confirming that there was in fact an heir to Hamish's estate. Unknown to anyone it appeared that years ago, when Angus was just a small boy, his eldest sister, Bella had emigrated to Canada and was never heard of again. That is except for the letter to Hamish of course, which he never replied to. As it turned out that there was just one surviving relative, a retired spinster. Well into her eighties and, having no interest whatsoever in owning an abandoned farm in the Trossachs, she gave her authority for Hamish's croft to be sold.

Chapter Seventeen

Discovered

THEY DO SAY that fate moves in mysterious ways. Well that was certainly true in Frank Forester's case. A missed flight. A wet afternoon in Glasgow. An impulsive visit to an auction room and half an hour later he suddenly found himself the proud owner of a Highland croft. Thankfully, and much to his relief, when he returned home to London and gave his family the news, wife Paula and children Mabel and Monty were all delighted.

Three months later and with the sale of their London house completed, the Forester family moved to Scotland. As a qualified vet, Frank quickly found work at a practice in the nearby town of Callander. While his wife Paula, who had once worked as a nurse, endeared herself to the community by volunteering to work three days a week at the local hospital. Rather than renting a property while much needed repairs and improvements were carried out, the family decided to move into Hamish's old farmhouse and despite having to put up with a Portaloo toilet, draughty windows, no central heating and no television, Mabel and Monty were in seventh heaven.

At ten Monty was the youngest by two years but he was already a head taller than his big sister. Not that Mabel cared. Boys were supposed to be taller anyway weren't they? They both attended the same school and while it had taken a while to familiarise themselves with the local dialect, they had settled in well. As the only 'Redhead' in the family Mabel had always been a bit self-conscious about the colour of her hair. So you can imagine her delight when, during their weekly history lesson, the teacher had told the class all about the Scottish heroine Flora McDonald. How the flame-haired beauty had rowed her boat across the sea to Skye and, save the life of Bonnie Prince Charlie.

Unfortunately for the rest of the Forester family, Mabel also discovered that Flora's daring deed had been immortalised in song. It took her less than two minutes to learn the words of the first verse off by heart and if she sang it a hundred times, she sang it a thousand. Eventually, before she ended up driving the whole family stark raving mad, her father brought an end to her incessant singing by threatening to donate her pocket money to the RSPCA. Still Mabel didn't mind, the moral victory was hers. Redheads were cool and they always had been. Well at least in Scotland they were.

With both parents away in Callander choosing new units for the kitchen, it was the perfect time for the two children to explore the sheds scattered around the croft. Sadly the first one contained nothing but items of old furniture. The next three they looked in were no better. Each of them piled high with junk from floor to ceiling. With just one shed left to explore they made their way up the hill. Much to their surprise when they tried to open the door they found the shed was locked. Miffed at not finding anything mechanical he could tinker with,Monty was more than happy to call it a day. It was probably full of old rubbish anyway, just like all the others he said. But Mabel wasn't one to be put off so easily. There had to be a key somewhere and, she was determined to find it. So, ignoring Monty's long face, she turned on her heels and began running back to the house. Half an hour later, with her mop of red hair covered in cobwebs Mabel emerged in triumph from the cupboard under the stairs and clutching the brass key in her hand, she raced out the farmhouse door.

Surprisingly, the key turned easily in the lock and, pulling open the heavy door the two children peered inside. Although the interior was quite gloomy, once their eyes became accustomed to the lack of light, they knew instantly that they had discovered an Aladdin's cave.

'Wow!' Exclaimed Monty, 'now this is more like it.'

Stepping inside, the pair stood for a moment staring in disbelief at the extraordinary treasure-trove of objects crammed into the small space. In the centre of the shed, surrounded by a wall of cardboard boxes stuffed full of books and magazines, stood a huge wooden table. Covering most of its weathered surface were copper kettles and pans of all shapes and sizes, their once bright surfaces, now dull and tarnished. The remainder of the space was taken up by piles of assortment biscuit tins and dozens of coffee jars filled to the brim with nuts and bolts. All coated in a thick layer of dust.

Precariously balanced on top of all this ironmongery was a glass fronted display case. Perched inside it on a branch, was a rather sad looking long-eared owl, with one of its eyes missing. Securely attached to three of the walls by metal brackets were wide wooden shelves, each one groaning under the weight of china tea sets, dinner services and brightly coloured vases. Most surprising of all though, were the rows of ornate lamps and crystal chandeliers suspended on hooks from the ceiling. Their cut glass prisms covered in a gossamer veil of spider's webs.

Wherever Mabel and Monty looked, every inch of space was crammed full of objects Hamish had collected over the years.

'Why would anybody want to collect all this stuff ?' said Mabel, quite bewildered by what they had found.

'Search me,' replied Monty, running his eyes over a magnificent cast iron Victorian fireplace which was propped up against the wall. 'Perhaps whoever put them here was planning to open a junk shop or something. I'll bet some of this stuff is pretty valuable.'

Mabel didn't answer him. Something had caught her eye. Curious to get a better look, squeezing between piles of wicker baskets, balanced precariously one on top of the other, she made her way towards the far corner of the shed.

The Watling Rol-A-Top was just were Hamish had left it all those years ago. Although strangely the tarpaulin sheet covering it didn't have a speck of dust on.

'What have you found?' asked Monty, seeing Mabel making her way towards the far corner of the shed.

'I don't know yet,' Mabel replied, 'it's covered over.'

'Well whatever it is you'd better leave it alone,' said Monty, concerned that Mabel might go and injure herself.

'It's all right,' said Mabel, 'I just want to take a peek.'

Knowing that no matter what he said his sister was going to do what she wanted anyway Monty shouted back;'Well just be careful that's all.' Smiling at Monty's concern for her safety, apprehensively Mabel reached out a hand.

No sooner had her fingers touched the sheet of tarpaulin, when deep inside the One Arm Bandit a series of gear wheels began slowly rotating. Their rows of teeth interlocking with the precision of a Swiss watch. At first nothing appeared to be happening. But then as the wheels began spinning faster and faster, a spring attached to the arm of the pay-out lever began tightening and then as if by magic a shiny silver coin slid silently into the pay-out tray.

APPENDIX

SUTTON HOO.

In 1939 a Mr Brown did discover an Anglo Saxon burial ship at Sutton Hoo and with it probably the most exciting treasure trove ever discovered in the United Kingdom. Among the finds were a warrior's helmet and shield both of which, together with other exhibits, are on display at the British Museum in London. As no body was ever discovered, only evidence that there had indeed been one, there is much speculation as to exactly which Saxon King was buried there. Many think it was Raedwald but in my story I have offered the possibility of it being Aethelhere. Of course nobody will ever know for certain who really was buried there but regardless of this, the site at Sutton Hoo offers a tantalising glimpse into our nation's history and is well worth a visit. www.nationaltrust.org.uk/sutton-hoo

BATTLE OF THE LITTLE BIGHORN.

Probably better known as 'Custer's Last Stand' this was to be the last and defining battle between the US Military and the Plains Indians and although it ended in a victory for the Indians, ultimately it was to lead to their downfall. On that fateful day, Captain Myles Keogh did in fact ride a horse named Comanche and although there were probably other cavalry horses who survived, these would have been taken by the Indians as spoils of battle but because Comanche was badly wounded he was left to die. Except of course he didn't and when he was rescued two days after the battle he truly was the sole survivor of the battle of the Little Bighorn. Such was his fame that when he died he was buried with full military honours and his remains were sent to the University of Kansas where he is on display in their Natural History Museum. So if you ever find yourself in Kansas City, please go and pay him a visit, I know he would love to see you. www.biodiversity.ku.edu/exhibits

ALSO BY BARRY COLE:
THE CONQUISTADOR'S HORSE

The Conquistador's Horse is a combination of fact and fiction woven together into a captivating story about a boy and a horse and, how a tribe of Indians came to acquire their first horses.

When Tall Bull and the Cheyenne hunting party crossed the Arkansas River, and entered their enemies hunting ground in search of buffalo, little did they know that others were also crossing the same river. Fierce looking men armed with bows, spears, and war-clubs, their upper bodies and faces daubed with paint. They were a Pawnee war party returning to their village after a raid against their sworn enemies the Sioux. Last to cross the river were men on horseback. Pale-skinned men armed with swords, and muskets. They were Spanish Conquistadors, and they had come in search of Quivira, the city of gold. Soon the paths of all three would cross, and when they did, Tall Bull would discover a creature that he had never seen before, an animal which would haunt his dreams, and one day change the lives of his people forever.

There is also a bonus story at the back of the book entitled: *The Birth of the Wolf Clan*. A magical story full of evil spirits and shape-shifting.

Available from www.troubador.co.uk Price: £6.99

Printed in Great Britain
by Amazon